I Followed Jesus Straight To Hell

A love story

By RJ Young

First edition.

Copyright 2012 by RJ Young

rjyoungwrites.com

This book is a work of fiction. The characters, places and situations depicted in this work are a product of the writer's imagination and are not real. Any resemblances to real situations or persons living or dead are purely coincidental. This work may not be reproduced in any way without the author's written consent. All rights reserved.

Book One:

Cold Feet

ONE

There are two types of reporters in this world — failed novelists and everybody else. Unfortunately, I happened to belong to the former group. You could have called me a nebbish in that regard. Nebbish: a Yiddish word meaning, "never been laid."

Fuck.

Midway through my college career I could lay claim to being both poor and unfortunate, especially in pursuit of (literary) eternal life. Once those first three or four form-letter rejections came in, I began to look for other ways to put my professional writing degree to work. It wasn't until after someone — not the president of the University of Oklahoma, mind you — handed me my diploma that I found out there were only a few places my degree was actually valid other than the local coffee shop. So I did what most college graduates my age do — I moved back in with my parents.

It took a little less than six months for my parents to get tired of me shacking up in my old room, raiding their refrigerator in the middle of the night and writing stories that no one wants to read. I remember once coming home from a fruitless job hunt to find two items lying on my pillow with a note between them.

"Pick one," the note said. "You have one week to decide."

My father is nothing if not subtle. The first item was a recruiting brochure for the United States Marines Corp. The second item was a job application for the Norman Sentinel.

I'm a writer, not a fighter. Still, I thought I should at least hear my old man out. I mean, he was my (abusive and alcoholic) father.

"Why these two?" I said.

"Because your mother wouldn't let me ship you to seminary. And murder is a sin." My father cracked his knuckles to let me know he was serious.

"So you chose these instead?" I said, holding the USMC brochure and newspaper application in each of my hands.

"At least if you died in combat, you'd die a man. And I'd know I had raised one."

Maybe I chose it to spite my father — or because guns made me queasy. But journalism seemed like a great fit at the time because some nice lady in a bright evergreen and gold sundress at the Sentinel's human resources office thought enough of my wrinkled khakis, dingy shirt and light blue tie to hire my desperate white ass. The woman took two looks at my résumé, glanced at my clips from The College Daily and put them all in her briefcase.

"We'll be in touch," she said.

I don't know why I sweated while waiting to hear from her. Maybe it was because I was still gullible enough to believe people actually meant they would like to talk to you again when they say, "We'll be in touch." Three days after that interview I became a real live reporter at a real live newspaper.

Yippy skippy.

But seriously, many of the world's most prolific and innovative novelists started out as newspaper reporters. Not to mention it was the only way I could afford to pay my rent. Leave it to my old man to hike up my rent every month by an exponential rate — I am sure that was illegal now that I think about it — just to force me out of the house. And by the way, it worked. I was moved out of my parents' house and into a studio apartment in Norman in no time. Not surprisingly there was a $300 drop in my monthly rent.

Upon arriving for my first day at the Sentinel, I was given the city hall beat with an expressed mandate to smoke out all municipal bad guys. I took to the job so well that the section editor found me another job on the lifestyle desk. Not two weeks later the lifestyle editor thought I was so good at my job that she found me a job on the sports desk. The sports editor either thought I was great at my job or too lazy or too disinterested — probably the latter now that I think about it — to promote me to another desk. So there I was. Some might ask how I wasn't promoted to a complete other line of work. I've always thought it was in my best interest not to bother myself with these kinds of questions.

Seven months later I was still at the Sentinel writing rip 'n' reads for food and writing fiction for me. It was just as well. At least at Thanksgiving dinner I could say I was employed, even if that meant I was supposed to have something really interesting to say about the Dallas Cowboys' game. Hopefully my family will one day remember I don't like football. But that notion may never die seeing as I had the bad sense to attend college at a school that is crazy about the fucking sport. But it was at one such sporting event that I had the bright idea to propose to June Summers.

She loved football, and I loved her enough to take her to the first OU football game of the season. Why a Sooners' game? Simple: As a student, I could afford tickets, and I knew a couple of the guys who worked the scoreboard during games. We worked it out so at the end of the first quarter they'd flash "Marry me, June?" across the scoreboard, and I'd be there with ring in hand. Yes, I am the asshole who asked his girlfriend to marry him via the Oklahoma Memorial Stadium jumbotron. Sue me. I'm a writer. Words come out of my fingertips better than they do through my oval orifice — but I tried anyway.

"Will you marry me, June?" I said. She jumped out of her seat and shouted, "Yes!" A wave of euphoria washed over me. I couldn't believe it was that easy.

June settled down in her seat like she hadn't heard me — because she hadn't. I noticed the people around us were finding their seats all at once too. Then, I checked the jumbotron. The Sooners had scored a touchdown and led the University of Tulsa, 42-7.

Fuck.

She did eventually say yes outside in the stadium parking lot. And she said she was happy to know I wanted to marry her. And then this: "It would have been so romantic if you could have done this with that big electric scoreboard."

It was then I knew God sincerely hated me with the frost of one thousand Winterfell winters.

The months of my engagement with June began swimmingly. She was just about ready to graduate from OU and accepted a job at West Norman High School teaching dance. She talked often about buying a house during those days, but I was just becoming used to the idea of being a working adult. I was still writing sports at the Sentinel, a job I was sure I could underperform my way out of some months ago, but there I sat. But I did have my own place along with central heat and air, food in the refrigerator, cable TV and all of my bills were being paid on time. For a man little more than a year removed from the safety net of a college campus, this kind of stuff is tantamount to bending titanium alloy with your bare hands. You feel invincible, superhuman even. Of course, you are not, but you don't know that until you are confronted with your own personal brand of Kryptonite. It turns out my Kryptonite came in the form of a matching sapphire satin bra and panties set, long brown legs, shiny black hair and the sex drive of a ravenous black swan.

It was 3 a.m. on a Friday night. I was lying in bed. June called because she knew I was still awake. I made the mistake of telling her I would be back late, which meant I would be up late, too. I should have taken my big brother's advice and told her I'd talk to her tomorrow, but that was not how things worked between June and me. We always told each other where we were going to be and when was a good time to call. I didn't see any reason to amend the unspoken agreement until later that night. (Note to self: Naps during the day are now a necessity, and don't answer phone calls after 1 a.m. ever again.)

In the time it takes a cell phone to ring three times I contemplated why I should not have picked mine up. It was not as if she would not call back, and it was not as if she wouldn't have left a sobbing, distressed message on my voicemail.

I let the phone ring until my voicemail picked up. I was relieved to see the missed call text on my cell phone screen. Then she called again.

I didn't want to be bothered with her. Not that night. Everything was going so well in the days before. The wedding rehearsal was great. The caterer had done a fine job with the food and was good enough to help June and I with the seating arrangements at the reception Thursday. By noon on Friday, I was caught up with all of my work at the Sentinel and had finally found time to write more of my novel for the first time in weeks.

I left my cubicle at the Sentinel at five o'clock that evening to meet up with my friends at Maguires. My brother, Chris, James and I did what two micks, a dago and a honky would normally do at an Irish pub: We drank a few pints, told a few lies and no one said a single word about my impending marriage. It was good night, and I was having fun thinking about it in bed — until my cell phone lit up again.

Maybe she had an emergency. Maybe she had set her apartment on fire after trying to cook pot roast for what I could only hope would be the last time. It hadn't been out of the question for her to call and ask me to drive to the drug store on Lindsey and 12th Avenue late at night either. And me being me, I would always go, even before we started dating. Damn me for going.

I remember once, on a 2 a.m. drug store run, I jokingly asked the cashier, "I bet you see a lot of guys like me bringing these things to the counter at this time of night?"

"Yeah," he said with a deadpan delivery. "I sell a lot of oh-shit-please-no-baby tests this time of night to you guys."

Why did he have to say you guys? I hadn't ever been you guys buying a pregnancy test. I had never had a chance to be you guys buying a pregnancy test. From then on, I took my business to the CVS drug store on Flood Avenue and Main Street.

The phone rang again. By this time I was awake from my phone's incessant ringing. I remember thinking just before I answered the phone that this might hurt a little bit.

"Hello," I said. I was groggy and annoyed.

"Mikey, I really need to talk to you," June said. She was crying so much. I could barely understand her. I tried to tell her to calm down, but she just kept on crying as if my telling her to calm down was her cue to turn the faucet on full blast.

"Can we wear the hypothetical hat for a moment?" June said through her tears.

"Hypothetical hat," I said in an acquiescing tone. I hated the hypothetical hat. It had never been a good look for me.

"And remember," she said, "I'm not talking about you when we're wearing the hypothetical hat. Okay?"

Bullshit. We're always talking about me when we're wearing the hypothetical hat.

"Okay," I said.

"I made a mistake," she said. "I don't love him. I thought I did. I mean, I still do. It's just that I don't love him like that. I love him like I love my best friend. I love talking to him and being around him, but I don't love him like that."

Why couldn't I have just let the phone keep ringing? Fuck me. That's why.

"This marriage stuff is not for me," June said. "It fills me with depressing thoughts about love and my parents and how they're about to hit their twenty-fifth anniversary, that's the silver year, you know. They haven't had sex with anybody else for twenty-five years. That's a long time to be stuck with the same sex partner. They must have grown tired of each other by now, right?"

I remember wondering why she thought her parent's anniversary and sex life should impact her own, but that was the least of my worries.

"In less than nine hours me and this guy will be bound to have sex with each other forever and ever," she said. "What if he isn't any good at it? What if I'm not as good as I think I am?"

Yep, she did insult my lovemaking without ever having tasted the wares, in case you were wondering.

"I can't do forever, Mikey," she said. "I can't do it. Not with him. I mean, I should be able to, but I know right now, at this moment, that I can't and I don't know why I can't."

Why was a good question. Allow me to explain while donning the hated hypothetical hat: June had been seeing this guy for the better part of seven years, and they had been friends for nearly twice that length of time. They had been through high school together, comforting each other in their awkward teen years. They went to college together, and although they didn't start dating each other until later, they had been close friends all along. No one knew June better than him, not even her parents. Still, June decided in her bedroom — in the middle of the night — she didn't love him anymore. So knowing all that, I reciprocated the question of "Why?"

"I don't know why," June said. "I told you that already."

She was screaming into the phone. Considering June starts screaming when she becomes flustered and emotional while watching Project Runway, I was surprised she had not answered the phone with a Banshee mating call.

"It's not that he's not good enough or that I don't think he'll make me happy," she said. "It's … I don't think I'm good enough, you know? Like, I don't think I can make him as happy as he makes me. I know I'm not good enough for him."

That sounded like a cop out. And I told her so. It would have been one thing to fall out of love because she couldn't handle the commitment or because the thought of saying "I do" before a priest in the holy Catholic Church and in front of her friends and family was utterly terrifying. I could understand that. I had those thoughts myself. But it was entirely different to claim not be good enough for a man who had the wherewithal to propose. I mean, it was him asking her. No man would ask a woman to marry him if he didn't think she would do a damn fine job as his wife, lover and confidant. It just wouldn't happen. The universe doesn't allow such things. Or at least, it shouldn't. Again, these are all things I had to spell out in crayon for June. It was something I'd become used to doing over years.

"How do you know he loves me like you say he does?" June said.

"I just do. Trust me. He loves you. He really, really does."

"But what about when it gets hard?" June muttered through shotgun sobs. "What about when he gets tired of me? What about when I get, uh, emotional?"

Like right now?

Okay, I didn't say that, but I had to bite my cheek not to say it. What I did say was, "When it gets hard is when it is also the best. Sure it isn't ideal to live in a one bedroom apartment in the middle of an Oklahoma winter with no water and no electricity sometimes, but it wouldn't always be that way. There are hotter than Hell summers, too. That's when two people in love get to find out exactly what being in love actually means. That's when two people in love have to rely on each other for warmth and comfort. It could never get any worse than those two people being broke and alone together, and that's not bad at all."

She seemed to be listening to me. At least, I thought she was listening to me because I couldn't hear her crying anymore. I only heard her slow methodical breathing on the other side of the connection.

In one fell swoop, June had managed to scare me with a 3 a.m. phone call — a phone call that in college could have meant any number of things; all of them bad — cried incessantly and spoke to me with a tone of teenage hysteria that should only be invoked for a John Hughes film.

I figured she might have thought I was making sense, so I just keep talking. I talked about baseball cards, my favorite writers, and I even told her my Three Trees joke before I heard what I had been waiting for — a laugh. I was content not to know what she was laughing at. It didn't matter. June was laughing.

June laughing meant I was doing my job. And it usually meant we weren't too far from hanging up the phone. I would have been grateful for that. When I last looked down at the clock, it read 5:03 a.m. It was supposed to be our big day today, and I needed sleep to get me through the wedding and reception. So in the interest of brevity and my own selfish attempt to get some much needed sleep, I asked, "So we're still getting married tomorrow, aren't we?"

The sound of her voice was muffled by loud sobs, sniffling and snorting, but I was fairly sure I heard the word No — with a capital N — come through my phone.

"What?" I said.

"No, Mikey, we're not getting married," June said.

Shit.

"I had sex with another man," she said.

Fuck.

I had a right to be angry. I had a right to feel betrayed. Not only did the love of my life tell me hours before our wedding that she no longer wanted to be joined in holy matrimony with me, but she told me she had slept — no, not slept — she had sex with someone else. And it wasn't even a woman. I should have gone on a tirade. I should have yelled and screamed with everything I had through my damned cell phone. I should have told her she was a tramp, a floozy of the lowest degree, a woman who was probably directly related to Pontius Pilate's wife. I should have told her if not for my roots as a good Catholic boy — I was an altar boy for Christ's sake — that we would have done the deed back in high school while she was still vulnerable. Or maybe I should have told her I could be just as daring and dangerous and promiscuous as the next STD-laden dick. I should have told her I hoped she caught something so viral and violent that it ate out her ovaries and made her ooze a greenish liquid from her hairy snatch. But I couldn't say those things. I couldn't tell the woman I loved to go jump off a cliff because that would have meant I would have had to follow.

We Catholics are on some other shit when it comes to contemplating marriage. The Pope and his Cardinals do not recognize divorce, and so by extension neither do his followers. So we good Catholics think long and hard about the people we want to marry. I wish my parents had just raised me and my siblings to be Southern Baptists — they don't feel guilt at all, and I'm quite sure sex is celebrated as a divine miracle to be enjoyed with whoever and whenever possible.

"Mikey? Mikey, are you there?" June said.

I couldn't believe I hadn't hung up the phone yet. This baffles me even now. But I couldn't sit there in bed just breathing madly into the phone. I mean, I could have, but where would that have got us in the story? Probably not where we are going I can assure you.

"Yeah, June I'm here," I said.

"Well, say something about this." Her fury was audible.

"So if we had been fucking all along, we would still be getting married?"

A valid question, I thought.

"Is that all that you're worried about? That I had sex with Jake?"

Well what the fuck else should I be worried about? That's all any man would care about, especially those of us who have lived most of our lives as pure as the Virgin Mary. But that thought was overtaken by the mention of his name. I knew a Jake, Jake Mishkin. He was a prick. In fact, I would go as far as to say he was yet another nasty, white pimple on the hairy ass that is my life.

"Who's Jake?"

"No," June said.

"Who is this asshole?"

"Stop it."

"Was it Jake Mishkin?"

"I shouldn't have said his name."

Damn right she shouldn't have said his name. Guys don't forget the names of the fellas who are boinking their fiancé on the side. But Jake Mishkin? I can't stand that asshole, and she knew that. This is the same guy who had been picking on me since my middle school years at Alcott. Mishkin was a stockbroker in New York City. He probably opened an IRA on my lunch money alone.

"Why him?" I said. "When did you guys first get it on? Where did you do it? How was he? Is his dick twelve inches in length or circumference?"

"Stop it. You're being ridiculous about this."

"Fine, I am willing to forgive you of your transgression and move on."

That was me trying to salvage what is left of our engagement in my own condescending way. That's another trait of Catholics: We will try to fix anything — even Nazi Germany — if you let us.

"No, Mikey, I won't marry you."

June hung up the phone. I dropped my cell phone on the bed beside me and thought about what had just happened.

I wished I was still wearing the hypothetical hat.

When I showed up to the cathedral later that morning, June's father, Bob, or Mr. Summers as I called him, was sitting on the church house steps. He held a lit cigarette between the index and middle finger of his right hand and a bottle of Jim Beam in the other. An open box of Krispy Kreme donuts sat on the steps beneath his feet. I walked the length of the sidewalk up to him.

"You look a little over-dressed," Mr. Summers said.

I looked down at myself. My tuxedo was wrinkled and my tie was unbound. "Well it was her idea to do the big, formal, family wedding."

"I'm sorry about that," he said. He took a swig of his whiskey and handed me the bottle.

I took the bottle from him and drank deep. "I thought I'd make the trip, you know, just in case I didn't hear what I am now sure I heard when I spoke to her last night."

Mr. Summers smiled at me and reached for a pack of cigarettes, which sat beside the donuts.

"Cigarette?" he asked. Mr. Summers held out the box to me.

I reached for the pack of cigarettes and took his lighter from him. I shook out a cigarette and lit it. I blew out the smoke easily, letting the nicotine take full effect. "I quit smoking when we got engaged," I said.

"Rebecca made me quit when we got married."

"Why are you smoking now?"

He laughed. "I got married. I've had cold feet ever since."

"What has kept you married to Mrs. Summers for so long?"

Mr. Summers leaned back on the church steps and took a long, contemplative drag from his cigarette and blew out. He dropped the cigarette on the cement steps and crushed it out with the heel of his work boot.

"You know, I have been known as Bob Summers all my life. Folks around Noble know me as Bob. When I went to war, folks called me Bob. When I came home and took over my daddy's farm, folks called me Bob. Even when I was kid working as a cowhand for old man Riley up yonder off Highway seventy-seven, folks called me

Bob. Hell, I think you're the only person in God's kingdom who calls me Mr. Summers. But Rebecca Mary Wafer Summers remains the first person to ever call me by my government name. Do you know what it is?"

I looked up from the ground and shook my head. "What is it?"

"It's Marion Robert Summers III," he said proudly. "And damn if my wife isn't the only person over three counties who can get away with calling me Marion without receiving a bullet in the back."

I had no idea what he was talking about. He must have known I didn't because he put his hand on my knee, looked at me and said, "You have to respect a woman who has the gumption to call you by your government name. Those women come strong, come sturdy and don't scare."

"Did my daughter ever call you by your government name?"

"No sir," I said. "She just called me Mikey like everybody else."

Mr. Summers held my gaze for a few moments and then picked up the pack of cigarettes I had left on the ground. He lit another one and blew out.

"Well, son, I'm sorry it couldn't be my daughter, but I hope you do find one that will readily call you Michael without thinking twice. Something tells me you're going to need a woman like that in your life. And one more thing," he said, "I liked you best of all of the boys June brought home. That puts you somewhere between a sopping wet cow turd and the maggot that eats it."

"Thank you, sir, I think."

"You're welcome, boy. You're welcome."

I would have loved to have been Mr. Summer's son in-law. The man had always treated me fairly and with respect, which is more than I can say for my old man. Mr. Summers was always willing to listen to me babble about writing, work and his daughter, though I think he kind of liked the daughter part. Even when June and I were not dating, Mr. Summers used to have me over to his house to talk on a regular basis. He was smart enough to figure out I didn't have too many friends, save his only daughter. We sat on the steps looking into the blue sky. It was the first time in a long time that I wished it would rain. I wished the color gray would take over the sky. I wanted legions of clouds to block the sun from view and those birds to quit their incessant singing. But it seemed clear that the universe was happy to see me made up in my tuxedo, ready to be married and looking the part of a fool. So it was no surprise to me when my brother pulled up in his Corvette to St. Mary's steps.

My brother, Ron, stepped out of the driver's side door. He, too, was wearing his tuxedo, though his collar was undone and he had on his favorite black sneakers.

"Hi, Bob," Ron said with a half-wave. "Your daughter didn't change her mind again this morning, did she? Because I am growing tired of her shit." My brother never liked Mr. Summers, and today he was letting him know that fact.

"Ron," Mr. Summers said, acknowledging my brother, but not his quip.

"Mom and dad want to see you at home," Ron said to me. "They're afraid you might do something stupid. Again."

"Stupid like what?" I asked.

"Like go to the bar and drink yourself silly or try to marry that black b—," my brother stopped mid-sentence. He glanced at Mr. Summers. Mr. Summers cut his eyes at Ron. I could feel the tension building between them. And there's nothing like the tension of potential interracial in-laws.

"Well let's go home and assure them I have not done any such thing," I said, trying to head off the fight I could feel coming.

"And then we can go to Maguires," I added quickly. That drew a smirk from my brother.

"I've got some mouth wash in the car to get that smell off your breath."

"I haven't been drinking."

"You know we Irishmen can smell whiskey from across the Atlantic," Ron said. "Don't lie to me; just drink the mouthwash quickly. Besides it's not the whiskey I'm worried about. I know you can't hold your liquor for shit, little brother. You probably vomited twice on the way here."

Three times, actually.

Ron turned around, not saying goodbye to Mr. Summers, and walked back to his car.

"Thanks for meeting me here, Mr. Summers," I said. "I always appreciate a chance to talk with you."

"You're welcome, Mikey. Go on home now."

"May I have a donut first?"

"Sure."

I grabbed two donuts and devoured them each in five bites. I waved goodbye one last time to Mr. Summers, dropped my cigarette to the ground and crushed it out.

As I walked to my brother's car, I thought about what I was going to say to my parents — my extremely religious, extremely white parents, extremely prejudiced parents — and how none of what came to my mind was going to be a suitable enough explanation for them. They never liked the idea of me marrying out of the faith, and they liked it even less that I'd planned to marry a black woman.

My family is not just Catholic, we're Irish Catholic, and that comes with certain expectations. We are expected to endure stress and channel grief better than the rest of the world. Of this I have no doubt. It has been an uncontested fact in my family that when something goes wrong, we drink. And make no mistake — Saturday morning had gone terribly, terribly wrong. That's why it struck me as odd when I heard that my mother had asked my brother to make sure I had not been drinking. My brother was right. I can't hold my liquor. She had to have known by then I was going to slug back a few, or maybe she only hoped to have me sober enough to deal with my Pappy and his shenanigans when in reality it would probably be best if I was smashed.

Pappy has stayed with my parents since I was eight years old. My parents tried once to put him in a nursing home, but he wouldn't have it. Once they forced Pappy into an assisted-living community just outside of Tulsa. Damn if that old codger didn't succeed in getting himself thrown out just four days after ranting about how he "didn't want no fucking darkies poisoning his meals." My Pappy: champion of the Civil Rights Movement.

According to Pappy, Irishmen are the true slaves who built this country. He has no problem telling me — or anyone else for that matter — about how hard the McNulty family has had to work since coming to the Land of Opportunity. For Pappy, it was an opportunity for his father before him and his father before him to break their backs for little to no pay for the chance that their children and grandchildren might have the kind of rights and opportunities that were stripped from our people in the Old Country. (I used to get an earful of this sort of talk every time I brought home subpar grades or gave up a sport or quit while losing at a board game. I guess it worked too. It got to the point where I would rather get my ass kicked in football or lose badly in a game of Scrabble than hear Pappy complain about how I was pissing away everything my family and relatives had worked so hard to provide for me.)

Most families had to build a life from scratch once they crossed the pond, even going back to the forefathers of this nation. But Irish-Americans are a special breed. Every Irish-American who clings to his ancestry in primordial fashion is equally balanced with a chip on each shoulder. This leads me to my brother, Ron, the chippy one. He was christened Moran Ronald McNulty IV and is built like an action figure. He also has the emotional capacity of a red-nosed terrier pit bull off its leash. He is the oldest child. With the suffix my parents levied on him came the burden of not only my father's name, but the two McNulty men who preceded him. In my family, it's a lot to ask of a man to carry on his father's name. It means not only that you must be an upstanding member of society, but that you must produce a suitable, male heir to carry on the family legacy. Damn if my brother has not succeeded in every facet. It's just as well though. Had I been the eldest child, I'm sure the family line would have ended at my birth, certain to ponder the depths of hell. But for their sake — and my own I think — The Big Guy knew better than to send me careering out of my mother's womb first. The man to my right was the first to descend from where no man had descended before.

"What have you said to mom about this?" I said from the passenger seat. My brother drove a 1973 Corvette Stingray; the last year Chevrolet produced that model. Its exterior was pearl white. He had the interior reupholstered and the engine rebuilt to its stock specifications. Thirty-eight years later the car runs like it just came off the assembly line. I pawed at its leather upholstery, nervously waiting for his response.

"A better question would be, 'What haven't you said to mom about this?'" Ron said. His large hand shifted the standard transmission seamlessly as we turned onto the highway.

"How is she taking it?" I said. "I mean, has she taken out the sherry yet or is she crying into an empty glass?"

"Oh, she was just breaking out the bottle when I left to find you," he said. "But that was three hours ago. Right about now I bet she's downing another glass, but I don't think it's her you should worry about."

"Who then? Pappy? Fiona?"

My brother stomped on the accelerator passing cars that had the nerve to drive the fifty-five mile per hour speed limit.

"Dad?" I said.

My brother looked over to me with a knowing eye. "The last time I saw him he had broken out the Jameson's."

Fuck.

My father only broke out Jameson's Irish Whiskey in times of unique crisis. Usually he was content to get sloshed on with the Black Stuff. On the third day of the union's strike at the steel mill in Norman in 1999, my father went through three bottles of Jameson's before 3 p.m. When my baby sister, Fiona, got pregnant without first going through with a Catholic wedding, my father became so drunk that my mother kicked him out of the house for two days. Then there was the day I told him I proposed to June. My father drank so much and became so angry that he screamed obscenities that would have made the Blessed Virgin shutter. I still have the scar above my right eyebrow from where he cracked the empty bottle of whiskey over my forehead.

"Yep, dad is well and truly lit," my brother said.

"He can't be that angry, can he?" I asked.

"I guess you'll just have to see for yourself, won't you?" my brother laughed.

"The hell did I do?"

"You decided it was a good idea to marry outside of us?" my brother snapped back.

"I couldn't marry inside the family, now could I? They have laws against that, you know."

"I'm not kidding. Dad didn't like it when you got engaged, and he sure as hell doesn't like it now that she has decided to break it off with you."

"Look, I love her," I said.

"Yes, I have heard you say that, but you knew our parents wouldn't stand for it and just when they had warmed to the idea of having her in the family she goes and calls the wedding off. They have a right to be pissed. And so do you. Still, you should have fucked her when you had the chance."

I knew he was going to eventually say something like that, but it still hurt. "Why does it matter that we hadn't had sex?" I said.

"Would you buy a cow if you knew the milk was bad?"

"Now you're calling my fiancée a cow?"

"Yes, I'm calling your ex-fiancée a cow. She deserves it, but you still haven't answered the question."

"Well I did ask her to marry me," I said. "That should be a sufficient enough answer to your question."

"Whatever, Mikey," my brother said. "Things aren't the same after you sleep with a broad — even if you are in love."

I thought about what he said and was content to leave the discussion about my sex life there and turn back to the problem of my parents. "I just don't understand why they are as hysterical as you've described," I said.

"You know why," Ron said.

"They have known June is black since we were in high school," I said, hoping to head off his attack. "They didn't start acting strangely until I told them I proposed to her."

"Bingo."

"It's not enough that we're the only Irish Catholic family in this city. We have to be a racist bunch of Irish Catholics, too?" I said.

Ron shook his head. "No one would know that if you hadn't gone and tried to marry a black woman."

Ron had a point. Between me and my siblings my parent's racial prejudice was common knowledge, but among our friends and family it was a closely guarded family secret. My parents didn't have any black friends and didn't exactly encourage me or my siblings to have friends who weren't white. It's not as if they discouraged it either, but I remember my parents were less than thrilled when I told them about June. I remember my mother's face being agape and my father slowly walking toward the liquor cabinet.

"You got any good music in here?" I said. "Any Jay-Z or Kweli?"

"No, I don't have any of your jungle bunny, hippity-hoppity shit in my car. Good Christ, I worry about you sometimes."

I put my head down, thinking how much more my brother would know about the world if only he would let me play Thugz Mansion for him.

"You should also know Pappy has been drinking too. He can't wait to light you up." A smile slowly crept across Ron's face. At the time, I thought the day couldn't get any worse. I was wrong.

TWO

We pulled off the highway onto a two-lane road that led to the rural residential neighborhood that had become standard in cities with wide open spaces around them. Mom and Dad lived in Noble, just south of Norman. It's a nice enough town, Noble. It's nowhere near the size of Oklahoma City, and it's still too close to these Sooner crazies for my taste, but it's where my father wanted to call home after my brother graduated high school. I wished he would have picked somewhere less . . . rural. My father spent his days retired from the mill at the Elk Lodge. My mother decided she had had enough of babysitting everybody else's rugrats after twenty-seven years of teaching first grade, and my older brother and little sister had done their part to leave the nest.

When my parents moved to Noble, I'm sure they believed their children would never have need of their roof ever again once we all left for college. How silly of them. They must have briefly forgotten I am their flesh and blood — the resident family fuck-up — and my sister had a mind of her own. While I was entering my final year of college, my brother was finishing his MBA at Texas and about to start his job as an investment banker in Dallas. My sister had just graduated high school and was two years away from forsaking her scholarship and dropping out of Columbia. Ah, memories.

Ron and I stopped his car in front of our folk's house. It's a conventional two story, three bedroom home complete with a wide circular drive way that comes to a pinnacle in front of the house's front door. The driveway is adorned with track lights, beautiful roses, bright violets and gorgeous ferns. It's just begging for cars and trucks to park on it, but no, there was not a single car parked on the concrete. Instead, three cars and five pick-ups littered the front yard. We have lived in Oklahoma far too long.

While I covered my face thinking how awful it might have been to bring June and her family to my parents' home for the wedding reception, Ron did my conscious and his '73 Vette a service by parking alongside the curb.

"You ready?" Ron asked after putting the emergency brake on.

All I could say was . . . well I never received a chance to say what I was going to say because, well, I vomited.

"Christ, little brother," Ron said while throwing up his muscular arms. "Couldn't you have opened the door before blowing chunks all over my fucking dashboard?"

"I'm sorry," I mumbled while vomit dripped from my chin.

"Goddamn it, I swear on everything good and holy if you didn't have all those fucking freckles and horrendously bad luck no one would ever mistake you for Irish. You can't hold your liquor for shit."

"Why are you telling me things I already know?" I said. "Do you have any napkins in this panty-dropper?"

"Open the glove box under the dripping bits of Jim Beam and whatever the hell that is you decided to eat with your whiskey."

"Krispy Kreme," I said.

"What?"

"Krispy Kreme donuts, that's what I ate."

My brother shook his head in disbelief and got out of the car. I opened the door and sat with my feet outside the car. I wiped off the bits of half-digested glazed donut. He made his way around the front end of the car and leaned against passenger side of the hood.

"You want a cigarette?" Ron said. He took out a pack of Kools and offered them to me. I took one out of it, and he handed me his lighter. I inhaled the sweet poisonous fumes and gestured with my lit cigarette. "You know scientists have been telling us these things will kill us since birth," I said.

My brother took the pack back and lit up a cancer stick of his own and let the smoke float from his mouth slowly. "Yeah? I sure as fuck hope so."

I could not help thinking the same thing.

"Now about this June business," my brother said, looking at my parent's house and flicking the cigarette away. "Is it true she called this shindig off just last night?"

"At around 5 a.m. this morning actually," I said.

"And you had no idea this was going to happen? You had no clue? You didn't see the signs?"

"No Nostradamus, I didn't see the love of my life expelling me from her warm embrace and leaving me here with you to contemplate the pain that still pierces my soul."

"Will you stop with that lover's lament shit? You are a sports writer — not a novelist. You could at least use exhausted clichés to make your point."

Yes I am a sports writer, but he didn't have to remind me. He does this when he's trying to get under my skin. I dropped the cigarette and crushed it out with my wingtips. "All I'm trying to do is explain to you how I feel and what I feel," I said. "This isn't easy for me. Am I not allowed to grieve the loss of my one true love?"

"Shut up, pussy. That's probably why she broke it off with you in the first place. She realized she was about to be forever hitched to a eunuch."

"At least I'm not some failed college jock still living out his high school fantasy."

"Fuck you. I play semi-pro ball as away to keep in shape."

"You could do that at your local YMCA," I said.

"And you could submit to the fact that your ex-fiancée left your scrawny, ultra-sensitive, pale, white ass because she couldn't deal with the pain of being married to you."

"How the hell do you know I have a pale, white ass? You been looking at the other guys' dicks in the locker room again?"

I shouldn't have said that. There are a lot of things you can say to my brother that he'd shrug off, that he'd forgive and forget. But since he was accused of being a "flaming, fruity faggot" by our father in elementary school he has learned to take insults about his sexual orientation to heart. Before I was able to shut my eyes and cover my face from sight, my brother's oncoming fist flew into my face, pummeling me back into driver's side of his car. He reached into the car, pulled me out and threw me into my parents' well-manicured, front lawn. I would have said I was sorry, that I took it all back, but that would mean he would have had to un-straddle me and stop punching me in the eyes, nose and ribs. I felt eleven years old all over again.

"Jesus, Mary and Joseph, Ronald, get off your brother," I heard.

From my upside-down, slightly dazed position I saw my mother hauling ass toward us through the front door of the house. Her long, navy blue dress swished back and forth as her rosary jiggled around her neck. Any other mother would have loudly scolded or even hit her adult sons with a wooden spoon while they rolled around in the grass tussling like 5-year-olds, but I was not lucky enough to be shat from the womb of one such mother. Just as my brother was about to lay another good one into my freckled-face, my mother reared back on her left leg like a hornet-stung mule and put her right foot through the center of my brother's chest. My brother — being the big, muscular man he is — did not fly back nearly as far as I would have hoped, but he did fall flat on his ass, which was good enough to stop him from pounding me into the sweet, dark oblivion that awaited me. I could see his pride was hurt a little more than his chest.

"Ma, he started it," Ron said as he sat up on the grass.

"I did not. He punched me first."

"After you blew chunks all over my dashboard and called me a faggot."

"I never called you a faggot."

"It was implied."

"Both of you be quiet," my mother said, "or I will finish what you have started."

We both shut our mouths and listened. In our house, my mother's spoken word is not to be challenged. Once I made the mistake of correcting her in front of one of her book club buddies when I was twelve. I think it was something as trivial as how many tomatoes she bought at the supermarket that day. I don't remember exactly how it happened, but I do remember the burning sensation pulsing in my lips after she popped me on the kisser. She once popped my brother in similar fashion when he gathered the nerve to argue with her over being grounded for — surprise, surprise — kicking my ass. My mother smacked him so good that to this day he flinches when my mother reaches out a hand toward his face.

"Ronald, what has gotten into you?" My mother stood just shy of five feet tall, but her chest, hips and legs suggested she was built like a mini-fridge.

"I sent you to find your brother on a day when he is sure to be in need of his family and what do I find? You, once again, punching the living daylights out of him."

"But ma he—"

"Don't you 'But ma' me, mister. You would do well to shut your mouth, get up off my grass and march your behind inside the house or, so help me, I will have your father beat your rear until it is as red as a freshly painted fire hydrant. And call Mary-Katherine. She wants to know when you'll be home."

"Mom, I'm grown. Dad can't beat—"

She popped him with a swift slap behind the head. "Inside," she said with an air of finality.

Ron grabbed his head in pain and headed for the house.

"And you, Michael," my mother said. "Do you know what kind of embarrassment you have caused this family? Have you any idea what people are saying?"

"The hell did I do?"

She popped me upside my head and once more on my ears. I winced from the pain.

"Don't bring your filthy mouth inside my home, Michael. You know the rules of my house. While you are here, you will respect them — married or not. Now get inside."

Rather than argue with her further and get my ass kicked by both my brother and my mother for good measure, I followed the direction of my mother's menacing finger.

The first thing anyone must do when entering the McNulty household is praise Jesus Christ. I'm not kidding. The Messiah hangs on his cross, staring you in the face as soon as you open my parent's front door. If you don't cross yourself in reverence, I'm quite sure you may be struck dead by lightning, or you would have to deal with my mother going on and on about Hell and the eternal damnation that awaits you in the afterlife for the duration of your visit. Trust me — you prefer the former to the latter.

I passed the tall, emaciated, painfully white, blue-eyed, long-haired freak nailed to the front wall of my parent's house and was immediately greeted by the sight of Pappy in his La-Z-Boy recliner, a glass of Jameson's in one hand and a beer on the nightstand next to him, and the Sooners were running across my dad's 54-inch flat screen TV. I walked around in front of my granddad so I could look him the eye, though my knees trembled as I walked.

"Hi, Pappy."

"Get out of the way, you're blocking the damn game."

I moved to the left of the TV, situating myself so I was in between the flat screen and the living room window that showed the front yard. Pappy stared at the TV a while longer, nervously sipping from his glass of whiskey every few seconds. The last time I remember Pappy drinking this nervously was when he tried to tell my siblings and me about serving in World War II. He was there at Pearl Harbor when the Japanese blew everything to smithereens. That is also as far as he got in the story.

"I heard my daughter-in-law had to save your candy-ass from another ass-whipping," Pappy said.

I shuffled my feet, not saying anything. It was best to just let him talk and with any luck the Jameson's would kick in, and he'd stop. I mean, it's not as if I could have told the senile old man to shut his kisser and leave me the fuck alone, could I? I mean, I guess I could have, but I like to think I'm a well-mannered son and grandson for the most part, which is why I let him get away with his next comment.

"First you let one of these darkies stand you up on your wedding day," Pappy said.

Right.

"And then you go missing for hours, giving your mother fits."

Why should she be in fits? It's not as if I climbed atop the Bizzell Library and threatened to jump?

"And finally she finds you outside the house getting your ass handed to you by Ronnie just like he used to when you were kids."

You said that already, old man.

"You know all of this could have been avoided if you could've just married a nice Irish woman like me and your father and your brother Ronnie. But a simple, white Catholic woman is no match for your Jungle Fever. What do the kids call fools like you? Wiggers? Yeah, that's it. My son raised a goddamn wigger."

I know what you're thinking, and it just isn't true. No, my Pappy has never donned the hood of the Ku Klux Klan. (Probably because they don't have a union.) No, my Pappy wasn't one of those stupid white guys in Selma, Alabama who brutally beat black men, women and children during a peaceful protest march. (Probably because he was working a double-shift at the mill.) And no, he wasn't one of the legions of rich, white men who benefited greatly from Reaganomics. (The man was a Teamster for Christ's sake.) But yes, he does believe Malcolm X was full of shit — before and after visiting Mecca. And yes, like most white men across America he believes O.J. did it.

When I was younger, Pappy complained that the Irishmen of this country were at fault for the eminent demise of the United States. He has furthered that assumption now that the President is black with a name that could never be mistaken for anything other than African in origin. He's an old man with a lot of pinned up frustration about the world — mostly that his wife is no longer here to help him deal with it. So yeah, I put up with his ass-backward thinking in a country that has at least made it to the point where we are legally equal, but that doesn't mean I didn't keep him as far away from June and her family as I could while we were dating. Look, I know my Pappy isn't an ideal human being, but I have to give him a lot of leeway. He taught me the proper way to sully a good Irish name: Drink massive amounts of alcohol on a Friday night, drunkenly tell everybody to "Go fuck themselves" on Saturday night and then wake up for Sunday morning mass, repent, confess and ask Father Jacob to say a special prayer for your colossal hangover.

"You know, back in my day, this kind of thing would not have had a chance to fester into the nightmare it is," Pappy said. "If you have to marry a colored woman, why not marry a spick? At least they're Catholic and can cook and clean. Or why not one of them chinks? You would have never had to worry about doing your taxes or balancing the check book ever again. But Civil Rights Act or no Civil Rights Act no self-respecting Irishman would've subjected his family to the kind of embarrassment that comes with being engaged to a black protestant."

Pappy ranted awhile longer, shouting down his ethnic slurs and vitriol from his La-Z-Boy throne. Soon, he tired of yelling at me, blamed me for missing the second quarter of the game and shooed me away. "Get into the kitchen with the women where you belong, wigger," Pappy said. "I can only hope your father beats the ever-living shit out of you for what you've done to my good name."

Thanks, Pappy. I love you too.

THREE

My mother sat at the kitchen table with a half glass of sherry in front of her, dejected and menstruation red with anger. My sister Fiona sat next to her, nursing a glass of water with her belly fully formed and ready to pop at any moment.

"That's just not how we do things," my mother blurted. "What happens when our family in New York hears about this?"

Oh no, not the family in New York again. I had to hear about the family in New York every time I did anything that might be construed as un-Irish-like. So naturally, I heard about the family in New York quite a bit.

"Your father isn't taking this well," my mother said.

"I can only imagine," I said.

She popped me three times as quickly as those three words can be typed. The woman has quicker hands than Bat Masterson.

"This is no laughing matter," my mother said. "You don't realize the kind of embarrassment you have brought on this family do you?"

Honestly. How embarrassing could my non-marriage have been? Had they forgotten it was me who had not only been left at the altar but told the wedding was off on a cell phone like it was some kind of high school break-up? I could see my mother's eyes beginning to well up, which was my cue to leave.

"Where is Dad?" I asked.

"He's in the back yard. You had better go talk to him."

"Off I go then."

I walked out of the sliding glass door and saw my father's cold shadow projected onto the warm grass. He sat alone in an old lawn chair. A glass of Jameson's sat idly on a wood table beside to him. As I stood in the entry way between the kitchen and the back yard, all I could think about was how much talking to my father about June was going to hurt.

Ron was my father's favorite, which means I've been shit out of luck since birth.

He's the child who was given my father's name. I'm the child who was given the first name of a serial killer. He is the athletic one. I am the uncoordinated mess. He has a wife, two kids and a mortgage he can pay on time. I struggle to pay rent on a one bedroom hole in the wall.

It didn't matter what my big brother did, he was always going to come out the better son just like John F. Kennedy's older brother, Joe Jr. At least JFK's big brother was good enough to, you know, die. Not my brother, though. With my luck, he'd live longer than Methuselah, and while my father watched from Heaven he would tell his father's father how proud he is of his oldest son. I'd be forgotten and probably left to burn for all eternity in Hell — still a virgin.

I stood in front of my father as he took in the afternoon sun. Though he was a lean 6-foot-4, his face was gaunt and his eyes were sunken into their sockets and bloodshot. He looked like he hadn't slept in weeks. I stared him in the face, not knowing what I should do or what I should say.

"You know your mother and I were younger than the two of you when we decided to get married," he said. "If I could do it all over again, I would have waited. We loved each other, yes, but your mother was also pregnant with your brother."

I shuffled my feet in the manicured grass. I noticed I was still wearing those Italian leather shoes. I glanced at my father's tired, chipped, steel-toe boots.

"We're Catholic," he said, "so our marriage was . . . accelerated.

"I know you have a job, and I am proud of you for that," he said. "That is worthy of the McNulty name. You have always been diligent in this writing, even though I think you're hard-headed. But that hard-headed attitude will get you through more rough times than you know. And that is worthy of the McNulty name. Should your woman have shown up this morning you would have married her. Before almighty God, Father Jacob, your family and the Blessed Virgin, you would have been joined in holy matrimony. No doubt you would have seen it through to the end. And that is worthy of the McNulty name."

I could feel my shirt getting wet with sweat and my cheeks flushing red.

"But have you thought about what your children would be? They certainly would not look like a McNulty. Have you thought about how you and that woman would be received in the world?"

"What is it with you people?" I yelled. "Yes, June is black and Baptist. Yes I'm white and Catholic. You have known this for years. Why is it such a big deal now? Why is it when I say I'm going to marry the woman I have publicly courted for years and then she gets cold feet that you are embarrassed and angry? Why? If anybody has a right to be angry it's me."

"Because you have sullied this family's good name," he yelled, "the McNulty name — my name."

He rose from his chair, and I felt the back of his gnarled and calloused hand strike me across my face.

"You let a darkie — a nigger — dupe you into committing to the holiest union in the world and then allowed her to back out of it, leaving your family to suffer this, this embarrassment."

He slumped back into his lawn chair. His chest heaved with discontent and anger for me. I thought it best to walk away, to leave him to cool off. But I couldn't do that.

"Dad, I am not you," I said. "I never was. I know you like Ron best. I know that. And that's okay. But I love June. I will always love June, and if it angers you this much then I guess it is best we don't speak anymore."

I can't say I meant what I said about never speaking to my father. And yes, he had hit me many times before, but he always said he was sorry later. He rarely agreed with any of the things I wish to do — least of all, writing — but he has suffered them. My family means the world to me, but my love for June consumed galaxies. I hoped my parents would see that. Maybe one day they will respect me for it.

I sauntered back in from the backyard and saw Fiona sitting at the kitchen table. She met my eyes with a wry smile and shrugged her shoulders. Of all my family, my baby sister was the person who knew best how I felt about June and how it felt to be in love with her.

Fiona had fallen for some guy while at Columbia, an artist, and she told the family about her love when she first came home for Christmas Break. She said her beau didn't have a lot of money, but he had brilliant prospects — whatever that meant. Still, I could see she was in love. Her eyes glinted when she spoke about him. I remember hoping he wasn't a douche bag.

Like most beautiful women Fiona has a knack for dating douche bags. You know, not the kind of guys whom would hit a woman, but definitely the kind of guys who would not think twice when cheating on their girlfriend or wife.

It wasn't until later last year when she called me to tell me she was coming home I learned my petite, brown-haired, starry-eyed, little sister was knocked up and the guy who helped her get that way would not acknowledge the baby was his.

He refused to take care of the baby, refused to take care of Fiona, refused to love her.

See, douche bag.

I know. I never heard his side of the story, but Fiona was never the kind of girl to tell lies. When we were younger, she was the first one of the three of us kids my mother used to interrogate when one of us broke something because my mother knew my sister couldn't keep a straight face to save her life. So when Fiona told me how this guy had run out on her once he found out she was pregnant, I had to watch the tears streamed from her eyes.

When she begged me not to tell our parents, I didn't immediately understand. At first I thought she came to me instead of anybody else in the family because she knew I wouldn't judge her. It was only later, when she pulled out a picture of this guy that I fully understood why she came to me: He was a rather black, black man. Now, here I was on the other end of that conversation.

"Did she give a reason?" Fiona asked.

"Yeah. She said she'd fallen in love with somebody else."

"And you believed her?"

"Of course I believed her. She was crying and distraught and it sounded like she had been holding this in for a long time."

My sister cocked her head to one side, gave me a quizzical look and began to snicker.

"What?" I said. Fiona only did this when she thought she knew something I didn't. The trouble with this? Most of the time she did know something I didn't.

"You remember while you were off playing reporter at college June was a dance and theater major, right?"

"Yeah, so?"

"So, the woman knows how to dance and act. She's playing you."

"No, she's not. She called me wailing away on the phone, talking about hypothetical situations and shit. She'd made up her mind."

"Mikey, I love you, but sometimes you can be as thick as a steaming pile of bullshit. June's testing you."

"Testing me? I'm not taking my SATs here. I asked the woman I love to marry me and after months of engagement she declined my offer. So to hell with her test. I don't need it. And I certainly don't need the rest of my family telling me how much I've disgraced and embarrassed them over my failed engagement."

"If you honestly feel that way about June, then you don't deserve her. But you should know we girls can get cold feet sometimes. Sometimes we need to know it's more than just infatuation. Sometimes you need to actually tell us you love us. How many times did you tell June you loved her? Can you remember telling her you loved her when she called you this morning?"

"I didn't tell her straight out, no. But I told her in so many words. Mostly, I let her ramble on about a fucking hat."

"You might think about saying the words 'I love you' the next time you see her."

I thought about what Fiona said, letting it sink in, when my brother burst into the kitchen. "You ready to go to Maguires yet?" Ron said. "Chris and James are already there waiting for us. I'm buying."

That's my big brother: Beat me silly and then offer to buy me a drink. I walked over to Fiona, hugged her neck in thanks and left my parents' house for the only pub in town that served Guinness from a draft tap. I briefly forgot the devil's favorite hangout is also mine.

    Fuck.

FOUR

Maguires is a strange and wonderfully ugly hole-in-the-wall. It's a restaurant (read: really, really shitty bar) where the bartenders are nice enough to never cut you off when you're intent is to go on a night-long bender. They know when to talk and when to leave the bottle and you to hash out whatever problem brought you into their fine establishment.

I was first introduced to Maguires by some friends of mine I worked with at The College Daily. Since then, the ones of us who had no job and no future made it our hangout. My brother only goes to the pub with me when he's in town visiting the family. It's not his ideal establishment — my brother complained there weren't enough half-naked women walking around, and the place could do with three to five stripper poles in plain sight — but it was better than any of the other joints in Norman. I think a lot of that has to do with where the pub is in proximity to the university itself.

Maguires is located directly across the street from campus. I never realized how convenient it was to be able to stagger my pathetic skinny ass back to my university apartment — and later a house Chris and James and I rented — until I stayed a good ten miles south of it. It was nothing for the three of us to head over to the pub after making the next day's paper, throw back a few shots and drink a few pitchers of beer.

It is sacrilegious for me to have premarital sex with the woman I love and hope to marry, but it is perfectly acceptable — biblical even — for me to drink my ass silly, run around like a devious leprechaun and eventually pass out in the middle of the north lawn. Never change, Catholic Church.

We pulled up to the corner of Asp Avenue and Boyd Street, but when Ron saw how crowded the corner was with cars and people, he decided it was best to park five blocks down the road, right square in the middle of a vacant parking lot.

"You love this car too much," I said. "It's just a car."

"I could give two shits what you think, puke boy," my brother said. "Now let's go get you good and smashed."

We stepped out of the car and made the trek back to the pub. We walked in silence for the first few minutes. But I hate silence. And besides, I had to ask my brother a question.

"Do you think I love her?"

Ron kept walking with his eyes fixed on the pub's illuminated, gold and green sign. He would not look at me.

"Yeah," he said. "I think you do. But I also think you have terrible taste in women."

"That's a little harsh, especially since June is the only woman I have ever been involved with."

"Like I said, you have terrible taste in women."

"You're not saying that because she is black, are you?"

"No, I'm saying it because it's true, and in the end I want you to be happy."

"She does make me happy," I said.

"Are you sure about that? You've told me, repeatedly, you love this girl, but you haven't once told me how in love the two of you are. And she made it clear to you this morning that she does not feel as strongly as you do."

Fiona's words came rushing back to me. I thought about how this could have all been my fault, how I should have told her I loved her, how if maybe she'd have heard it verbally I would have meant something more to her. Before I could rebut my brother's claim we were met at the front door by Chris.

"If it isn't my favorite mick and his brother Ugly Mick," he said. "How the hell are you?"

"We're just fine, dago." I hugged Chris and began to walk inside with him. My brother followed.

"I can't believe you let him say that kind of shit to your face," my brother said.

"It's a special relationship, you know? Like Tony Blair and Bill Clinton." My brother shook his head in amazement.

Chris and I had been trading insults for years as a sort of running joke. At one point we decided we should think about stopping, but in the end we came to the conclusion that we enjoy making people feel uncomfortable.

We sat down at a table in the back of the restaurant where James sat with two full pitchers of beer and four glasses in front of each seat.

"How are you, Mikey?" James said. James rose up from the table and embraced me in a hug. It had been awhile since I last saw James. He took a job with the Associated Press a year after writing entertainment for the World in Tulsa, but he took some vacation time to come back to Norman for the wedding.

James was by far the smartest person at the table and my brother knew that. And it drove him crazy. James and Ron were classmates in high school. But James was just a bit better than Ron in nearly everything. He completed his journalism degree in three and a half years and spent the following semester applying to law school just to figure out he didn't want to be a defense attorney making hundreds of thousands of dollars. My brother called James an idiot in public for skipping out on law school and more lucrative career, but in private he envied James for having the courage to do what he could not. It was simply fate — and my stumbling into The College Daily newsroom one day — that made James my closes friend at OU. He was the one who originally encouraged me to propose to June. I was planning to thank him by making him my best man.

"How are you getting through this?" James asked.

"Like an Irishman," my brother shot back before I could speak.

My brother reached toward the middle of the table and filled each of our glasses to the brim.

"And that's why we're gathered here today," he said, "to celebrate the new beginning of a man who will not be doomed to the ball and chain like me; a man who will to howl at the moon whenever he feels the savage need. If only we could get him to let his peter do some howling too."

"It's a mortal sin," I said.

"So is not emptying your glass. So you had better drink up before God strikes us all dead. Wench!"

A petite redhead showed up with tray in hand.

In a trashy Irish accent Ron said, "Wench, I need four shots of Jameson's and a pitcher of the black stuff for me and me party."

"Guinness and Jameson?" Chris said. "Why the do we have to drink that nasty shit?"

"Because you are at an Irish celebration, goddamnit. Now shut up and drink."

"To your heart health, Mikey," James said.

We spent much of the rest of the night telling jokes, laughing about the good times we had shared during our years at OU. That was our way. When we were at Maguires the world didn't seem so harsh, didn't seem so bad a place to call home.

Then she came walking in. She sat down at a booth in the corner and I saw her order a single beer, probably a Corona. She always drank Corona. The stuff tastes like cat piss to me. But that was her beer, and I respected her for it.

After holding her in my gaze too long to be construed as casual interest my brother turned around in his seat to see what had caught my eye.

"How did she know we were here?" Ron said in amazement.

"Well it's not like she wouldn't know where we hang out," Chris said. "There was a time when she used have a seat at this table."

"Still, you'd think she would have found some other bar in town to have a beer," my brother said. "Oh fuck, she's ordering. What the fuck is that in her hand? Corona? Doesn't she know this is an Irish pub?"

"Why do you have to keep reminding us of your negligible ancestry, Ugly Mick?" Chris said. "We all know you're a redheaded bushy-top, freckle-faced prick."

Chris never liked my brother, but there weren't too many people walking the planet that Chris liked, and he was always going to be the one to tell you so.

"Look ass-wipe," Ron said. "My little brother may put up with your shit, but I won't. I'll snap your Italian ass in two if one more snide comment flies out of your blowhole."

"Try it, Ugly Mick."

My brother quickly stood up from his seat, and Chris reciprocated the gesture. Each of them was ready to knock the block off of the other. But even in my drunken state I acted the part of mediator. I stood up and placed my hands in each of their chests to separate them.

"Obviously, you guys have forgotten why you're here," I said a little tipsy off my ass.

"Yes, that would be because of me, I suspect," she said.

June stood right next to me, hands on her hips, purse over her shoulder and wearing that dangerously gorgeous smile of hers. I immediately sunk back into my chair.

"Who told you we were here?" my brother demanded.

"You've got a lot of nerve showing up here," Chris said.

"Well to answer Ron's question, James told me you'd be here," June said. "I thought Mikey and I should have a talk."

My brother, Chris and I looked over to James. He sat in his seat wearing a wry smirk, sipping his Guinness slowly. He put his glass down emphatically and got up from the table. "Well gents, I think it's time we called it a night," James said.

"I'm not going anywhere until this bitch accounts for what she has done," my brother said.

James walked around the table and placed his hand on my brother's shoulder and then Chris's shoulder.

"We need to give them time to talk," James said. He pushed Ron and Chris toward the door. I was going to follow them when James stopped me. "No Mikey, you're staying. You have some unfinished business to attend here," James said, gesturing toward June.

I again sunk down into my seat. June sat down in the chair across from me with a whimsical smile.

"I've been standing over there all night waiting for you to come over to my booth and talk to me," she said. "And all you could do was sit here and get sloshed with your friends. You're stupid."

"Excuse me," I said over the top of my half-empty glass.

"I said you are stupid."

"Did I miss something?" I said drunkenly. "Wasn't it you who called me at three in the morning to call off the wedding? And you're calling me stupid?"

"You have to understand… This conversation will have to wait until tomorrow morning. You're no good to talk to me now — you never are when you've had more than a single Guinness." June stood up from the table and grabbed me by the arm. "Come on."

"I'm not going with you," I said. I pulled my arm out of her hand and drained the beer left in my glass.

"Your ride has left you, and I don't think the bartender will not offer to drive a drunk home."

My face was falling asleep. I was sleepy, tired and stupidly drunk. I felt my right pant pocket for my wallet and realized it wasn't there. It must have slipped out in my brother's Vette and with it my cab ride home comeback.

"I'll walk," I protested.

"No, I'm driving you home." She set her jaw and cut her eyes at me. There was no talking to her when she got this way. It was her way — and there wasn't ever going to be a highway option.

"Okay, but I want to go straight home. No stopping for ice cream, or tampons at the drug store."

"Fine."

I followed her out to her Volkswagen Beatle and sat down in the passenger seat. The ride to my apartment complex was silent. She didn't say anything, and I was intent on keeping my mouth shut lest I shout to heavens once more how in love with this woman I was as I was known to do in an inebriated state.

June pulled into my complex and parked in front of my building. I stayed on the first floor, so at least she was not going to have to help me up the stairs. I stepped out of the car without uttering so much as a word and staggered to my apartment door. On the third try, I was able to finally stick the key into keyhole. As I turned the doorknob I felt a presence behind me. I turned around and June was standing right in front of me.

"What do you want? You gonna try to seduce me or something?" I said, jokingly.

June reached behind me, twisted the door knob and pushed the door open. She reached behind my head and pulled my face to hers. Her kiss was sweet, like licorice and caramel. She pulled back and looked at me.

"The answer to your first question is 'You,'" she said. "The answer to your second question is 'Yes.'"

FIVE

I won't lie. When June and I walked into my hole in the wall, I was scared shitless of what was to come next, which is to say if not for my natural anal retentiveness the contents of my intestines would have forcefully left my asshole with the thunder and rage of the Niagara Falls.

June had only acted like this once before and, at the time, she was the drunken one, and I was the sober person left to say no — repeatedly. Only after having the I'm-so-hopelessly-Catholic-my-penis-hates-me conversation again did she stop. But this time I was damn near out on my feet and in no position to refuse her.

We walked into to my bedroom, and she threw me down on top of my twin-size mattress. I hit the bed with a soft thud. I watched as she slowly pulled her purple dress over her head to reveal her matching sapphire bra and panties. She dropped the dress to the floor, and I looked down at the zipper on my pants. Even in my drunken state I was still able to achieve a hard-on. I couldn't help but think how proud my brother would have been of me during that moment.

June crawled on top of me and began unbuttoning my pants. She slowly pulled down my zipper and was about to put her hands in the pocket that lay at its center when I grabbed her hand at the wrist.

"No. I can't."

She ripped her hand out of my pants and sat up. "And just why the hell not?" she said. "It's clear he wants to play," she said, motioning to my raging hard-on.

"Yes, he wants to play," I said, gesturing to my pants. "He always wants to play. That's not the point."

"Then what is the point?"

June crossed her arms, still straddling my torso.

"The point is I don't want to have sex with you."

June made a slightly offended face and made a move to climb off of me when I grabbed her at the hips to stop her.

"Wait, I didn't mean it like that. It's not that I don't ever want to do this with you," I said, taking my right hand off of her hip to point to the large engorgement she was sitting on. "It's just that I don't want to do this until I get married. I wanted that person to be you. But you have other plans. I love you. Do you understand that? I really love you, and I feel that if you loved me you would want to wait because I have to wait. But you've made it apparent that you don't want to wait. I guess what I'm really trying to say is why did you have to go and *fuck* Mishkin?"

June's eyes welled up with tears, and she hastily tried to wipe them away. "I never had sex with him."

I sat up. I was drunk and confused and my face had obviously told her so.

"I know you don't like Jake — I've always known that. It was the only excuse I could come up with that I thought you might believe."

"But why did you need an excuse to call off our wedding? Why now?"

"I got cold feet. I was about to marry a man I had never lived with and never known on the highest intimate level human beings can achieve. Forgive me for reminding you, but you're the only virgin here among us. I know from experience that things change — even among longtime friends — after you have sex. I would have rather known that you do not want to be with me before we said I do than after. So I panicked."

"And you think the best way to say you're sorry is to crash my pity party and take me back to my apartment and jump me?"

"Actually, I thought we could, you know, do this and if you didn't want to marry me in the morning I could live with that."

"Wait, you still want to get married? To me?" I said.

"That was always my plan. But like I said, I got cold feet this morning. I love you, Mikey. If you still want to wait until after we get married, we can wait. And if we do this, get married and you want get our marriage annulled the morning after, we can do that too."

I couldn't *believe* this shit. To prove my love to the woman I wanted to spend the rest of my life with, all I had to do was lie in my bed and experience the deepest kind of intimacy two human beings can share together. But to do it, I had to go against the Catholic Church. But what if she was right? What if we did have sex, and I didn't want to be married to her after? I couldn't see how that was possible. But then again I was a virgin. And the one of the two us who was not a virgin in my bed assured me that it was possible. Was I going to trust the word of the woman I love, the partner that I hoped to be with me for remainder of my natural life, or was I going to trust the Catholic Church and its biblical text.

I reached my hand to her face and caressed her cheek. "This will be one hell of a confession."

"Father, it was unlike anything I have ever experienced before. It felt so good. And it lasted so long. We did it seven times in one night, Father — seven times." I sat in the confessional booth of St. Mary's with my rosary in hand.

"Go on, my son."

"I love her, Father. I really do. But I understand that it is a mortal sin to have premarital sex. I understand that. I'm sorry. I'm sorry for knowingly and willfully experiencing the greatest physical pleasure of my life. I will say any amount of Hail Mary's, Our Fathers and Glory Be's you tell me to. If there is a novena for what I have done to ask forgiveness, to repent, I will pray that too. But Father, I loved it. I loved every moment of it. Every scream, every squeal, the sweat, the drenched sheets, the smell of it — oh yes, sex is for me, Father."

"Calm down, my son. Calm down."

"I'm sorry, Father. What penance will you have me pray?"

"Pray one Hail Mary and one Our Father, and finish them quickly."

"Yes, Father." I recited each prayer quickly, holding the rosary in my hand. "Father, thank you for this."

"Don't thank me, Michael. Thank your bride-to-be for waiting for you to finish confession."

I smiled. I couldn't help thinking how much fun it would be to thank her that night. "Father, do you think I'll enjoy marriage?" I asked, still working the wood beads around in my hand.

"I think you will enjoy your wife, and she will enjoy you. That is what is important, Michael. Now, are you ready? Your guest will only wait so long. Many of them might be wondering if you have called off the wedding."

"Yes, Father. I am ready. I will be out in just a second."

"Not too long."

I heard him step out of the booth and the door shut behind him. I sat in my side and thought about the times I had spent with

June in the past. How much we had done together and the joy I felt knowing that in a just a few minutes time I was going to not only be able to call myself her husband but her father would be my father. My parents would become her parents. Then I thought about how easily she had lied to me about why she broke off the wedding and how she knew exactly where to hit me by using Jake Mishkin as cover. Then I got scared. I started thinking she might try to use Mishkin — or someone like him — against me in the future. Then I thought about what Mr. Summers had said, how June had never once called me by my christened name. I thought about how she manipulated me into consenting to have sex with her. I couldn't help it. I got cold feet. Where do I go from here?

Book Two:

God Is Spiteful

ONE

For most Catholic folks, the rosary is a tool to help us trudge and keep count of the four mysteries — Glorious, Joyful, Luminous and Sorrowful. We Catholics pray the rosary because it reminds us to 1) To pray every day 2) Who we are praying to 3) What we are praying for. I sometimes have trouble with the latter two, but I'll bet Mary Magdalene never had my issues.

The Blessed Virgin one day just miraculously appeared to Saint Dominic around 1214 A.D. and said, "Here, pray this" and left. There was no, "Hey how are you?" or "So, would you like to know when my son is making his second appearance on this cursed place you call Earth?" There wasn't even a "Hey, this Heaven place really is built on a grid with streets of gold. You should come check it out sometime." That chick just gave Dominic the words to the beads and left. In that way, I guess the Virgin is a lot like a woman who gives you herpes during a one night stand — it's an experience you must relive every single day of your life. But me being me, I pray my rosary the same way the Greeks use kompoloi beads — to physically demonstrate I am stressed out, and you should probably leave me the fuck alone. It's only an added bonus that my actions might please The Big Guy.

My personal favorite mystery to slog through is the Sorrowful set though for not the reason you think. No, I am not one of those crazies who believe in reciting the Sorrowful mysteries from Ash Wednesday to Easter Sunday, because the Pope said so. I am not one of those who believe the Sorrowful mysteries should only be spoken on Tuesday and Friday of each week (save those days from Ash Wednesday until Easter, of course). I am the kind of good Catholic who revels in the one driving force that distinguishes the ardent Catholic from the lax Catholic, the prayer-monger Catholic from the cover-Catholic, and in essence, the good Catholic from the bad Catholic. And that one driving force, was, is and forever shall be — guilt.

We Catholics love our guilt and punishment. We love to wallow in self-deprecation and self-pity. It's how we roll. Yes, I know Jesus allowed himself to be slung up on that cross, and he allowed himself to be tortured and humiliated in front of thousands for my sins — or so Sister Rita kept screaming at me. (Sister Rita could never prove what the man actually said and did. Call it the journalist in me, but even as a 6-year-old I had a hard time understanding why the son of the most powerful being in the universe, which scientists claim is infinite mind you, would subject himself to such ridicule and pain as Jesus Christ did. Sister Rita would just say I "had to have faith." Bitch.) For years, I pondered the motives of Jesus beyond what the Bible would have us believe, and it wasn't until high school that I started to see why the son of The Big Guy would do what he did: So no one on Earth would be allowed to bitch, moan or complain about their (perceived) plight in life.

You see, Jesus was a fucking *genius*. He thought, "Hey I know that these farcically feeble-minded cretins Pops created aren't going to be able to hold up under the stress of living on Earth, so I'll go ahead and take it upon myself to trump any excuses they might throw His way." (Jesus is a thoughtful motherfucker that way. Call it a side effect of being a product of the fruitful loins — adjusted daily — of the benevolent one true God.) So he said, "Yeah, let me go and live with them for thirty years or so, build up a great amount of wealth, perform a few miracles, form a gang — complete with a bookie *and* a doctor on call — and then allow myself to be thwarted by a Roman asshole with no backbone named Pontius in the most vile and wretched public execution imaginable. Then no one will feel good about bothering Pops — most of all on his self-appointed off day." And you know what? That shit worked. (On Catholics at least; there's no hope for those Southern Baptists. They'd be right at home in Sodom.)

So now every time I think I'm having bad day — a fucked-up-beyond-all recognition-kind-of-day — I try to get through the four mysteries of the Sorrowful. I usually don't feel much better after I get done, but it helps knowing the leading scorer for the New Testament All-Stars had to put up with a lot more shit than I did — or so I thought before I stepped foot into St. Mary's to marry June. I could have stayed in that confessional booth straight through the Second Coming, holding those fifty-nine wooden beads plus a crucifix and prayed straight through the Sorrowful. I would have been perfectly content to stay my narrow white ass in that dark sin bin just like a field mouse scared to enter the brave new world. And truthfully, that's exactly what I intended to do — Father Jacob's penance did not seem punishment enough — when I heard a sweet petite voice come through the shaded window of the confession booth.

"Mikey, are you still in there?"

It was June. I grunted in affirmation. I always grunt when I think it's better than saying exactly what's on my mind. Grunting was a lot better than saying, "Of course I'm still in here, and I'm seriously having second thoughts about marrying you, June. Could you go away? I'm trying to remind myself how much my life does not suck right now." So cut me some slack, okay? I was in a fragile position.

"You know, it's not just you that's scared. You are not alone, Mikey. We are in this together."

Funny how those words sounded oddly familiar. I can't tell you how many times I had to say the exact same thing to her. But at that crucial moment it was me who was turning out to be chicken shit. That' what my brother, Ron, would have called me had he been in that booth instead of June — a chicken shit. I wished he was there to call me a chicken shit. It would have been a hell of a lot easier to take being called a chicken shit than having the woman I asked to marry me trying to coax me into actually going through the act of, you know, marrying her. Shit, I was chicken shit.

"We don't have to go through with this," June said. "I told you that last night."

Yes, she had. And yes, I heard her last night when she said it. It was my idea to get married the morning after. I originally wanted this, or so I thought. But now something felt different. I felt different.

"I told you that you would feel different after we had sex, Mikey. If you want, I will get out of this box right now and tell them we decided not to do this . . . Yes, I think I'm going to tell everyone we're not doing this anymore." I heard June's booth door creak open.

"Wait, don't do that." The words just kind of slipped out. I hadn't thought about them before I spoke. They just came out.

"Well it seems awfully odd for us both to be sitting in here talking about this while everyone else sits in the pews waiting."

"Yeah, I know. I just needed to think about it a little while longer." That was as mildly as I could put what was going on in my head.

"You got cold feet, huh?"

How does she *know* this shit?

"That's okay," June said. "It's a stone that comes with the territory we staked."

"I guess. But I never thought I would feel this way about it, about you."

"Likewise. So are we still getting married, aren't we?"

"On one condition."

"I'm all ears."

"You have to call me Michael from now on."

"What? Why?"

"Just do it, okay? For me?"

"Okay, Michael. Can we get out of these things now? I think I might be claustrophobic."

Claustrophobia — the fear of being closed in; having no escape. Not the word I would have chosen at such a fragile moment, June.

Saying the vows turned out to be the easiest part of the entire shotgun proceeding. Father Jacob doubled as my best man. My about-to-pop-at-any-moment-sister, Fiona, served as June's maid of honor after I called and asked her to leave my parent's house under the guise of being hungry; a lie I was sure would turn out to be true later. In the pews behind us was a married couple June and I met on the way into the church as morning Mass let out. We asked them to sit and witness the wedding for us. The rest, as they say, was a piece of cake.

June and I left the church for a restaurant off Boyd Street close to OU's campus called The Bookstore. It was to act as our de facto dinner after the wedding, but in all honesty I was just hungry from the night before. Whoever said sex is its own nourishment is a bold face liar.

We pulled into the parking lot in my jalopy, got out of the car and made our way toward to the inside of the restaurant. The wood varnished walls have always been soothing to me, much like the inside of a bookstore. Go figure. The people that patronize The Bookstore are mostly students, but they are the same faces and people that you might find in the Bizzell Library on campus or with their eyes glued to the pages of a paperback novel while sitting on a bench along the South Oval of campus on a warm spring day. Maguires is the place for James, Chris and me. The Bookstore is strictly for June and I. Some places are sacred despite what Hitchens may have said. The restaurant where you and your new wife shared a pizza on your first date is one such place.

June and I seated ourselves, and a heavyset college-age female took our order. I had a pepperoni pizza and a domestic beer — they don't serve Guinness on tap. June ordered a vegetarian pizza and a cat-piss Corona. Dear God, I loved that woman, but if she ever tried to make me drink that urine she sipped, we were going to have to go back to being friends. Well, not really, but you get the idea. No man or woman in their right mind wants to suffer the watery taste of that shit. I know the commercials are cool — if not totally unrealistic — but you have to ask yourself, are you going to swallow that foul ammonia taste for the sake of looking cool? I surely hope not.

The conversation between June and I went well, which is one of the reasons I have wanted to marry her for so long. Any straight man can find a woman he is willing to have sex with. God knows I wanted June for a long time. And most men are able to find a woman who is genuinely less crazy than he thinks, though women are all crazy in one way or another — it's just about finding the kind of crazy you're willing to put up with for, you know, ever. While we men all want, and frequently talk amongst ourselves about finding the Perfect 10 — the one woman who is as smart as her breasts are big, who is as witty as her eyes are gorgeous and whose smile is as bright as her opinions are strong — the fact of the matter is you'd do well to count yourself as one of the luckier men walking the planet to find a woman who has even one of those attributes, and who is willing to put up with your constant shit on a daily basis.

Oh, whoops. Did I let the cat out of the bag? Did I just go against my gender in the war of attrition that the bean counters swear women are losing? I think I just accomplished both. And you know what? It's about time somebody did. You'd find out one way or another. I mean, God is a spiteful bitch. Yes, I'm an Irish-American man and that means my machismo should only be rivaled by the men who fucking invented the word. But it's time one of us men spelled it out for the rest: We aren't any fucking walk in the park ourselves. We cry. We bitch. We yell. We scream. The only difference between us and women is they have a bloody — and I use the word bloody deliberately here — excuse for their emotional outbursts. Men? We just want attention. So before you go thinking we have women outnumbered, that they have to come after us, remember they are more than able of comforting themselves (and each other, if you know what I'm saying).

Me? It's like I said before, I'm just ridiculously ecstatic to have found a woman I can hold a crazy beautiful conversation with over pizza and beer. Did I mention she is willing to put up with my shit on a daily basis and even went as far as to say so in front of a Catholic priest, in a cathedral named after a saint, in front of God and an enormous intimidating crucifix of Christ Almighty? Yes, you are correct to think I count my lucky fucking twinkle-twinkles every night.

But then there are the times I when the conversation turns to things I would rather not talk about. They are the times when I wish I could just hit the mute button on the remote control that controls my life. I don't normally have those kinds of conversations, specifically because I'm usually up to talk about anything, especially current events and books. (What else do aspiring novelists masquerading as working journalists like to talk about?) But June has always had a knack for making me want to stop talking completely. As a born rambler, that knowledge is hard to swallow, but it is true nonetheless. You see, I wasn't married to her for more than an hour and not through my third bite of delicious pepperoni pizza before June asked the question I was hoping to avoid for, you know, ever.

"So when should we tell our parents?"

"Never," was my first thought. There was no telling what appendage my mother might remove from me once she found out I was married in a Catholic church without my family in attendance and under the witness of perfect strangers.

"Do we really have to tell them?" I said. "Can't they just know we didn't break up?"

In the Land Of Man, that was exactly what would have happened. June and I would have lived happily ever after without the steely glower of parental discontent or need of parental approval. My word would have been enough, and the world would have submitted to my will done. But alas, I don't live in the Land of

Man. I live here. With you. In the Land Of We Must Tell The Parents.

"They are going to know something is up when they see another ring on my finger," June said. "And no, I will not take my wedding band off around your family."

There went my "What if" compromise, which again would have been perfectly logical in the Land Of Man. I took a hard swallow of my beer and tried my best not to contemplate what was to come next. June hadn't so much as laid a finger on her pizza and was nursing her Corona like there was a nipple on top of the longneck. Clearly, her mind was not on food.

"Well, we at least have to have a reception," June said. "Like a belated birthday party. I think that would be cute and a way to tell our parents thank you."

Yeah, a birthday party where my mother cuts my balls off and puts them in a jar over the top of the fireplace. That's about all the thanks I could have hoped to get. The alternative would have been the Cleveland County Sheriff's department locating my rank rotting corpse back in the woods somewhere along with a note folded up in my hand that read, "He married her without his mother in attendance. It was a righteous kill."

"It'll be fun," June said. "Just think about all the friends and family we could invite down. Not to mention they would not have to go through the boring ordeal of sitting through another wedding just to get to the cake and dancing. They could simply come down, eat and party."

"You do realize that wedding receptions cost money, right? I doubt my parents would be willing to put up coin for that after the wedding of your dreams didn't happen yesterday because someone got cold feet."

Yes, I was being a dick. It comes with my gender. Sue me.

"Don't take that condescending tone with me. I told you before that my mom and dad were more than willing to pay for the wedding, but you insisted that it come out of your pocket. I didn't know that out of your pocket meant out of your parent's savings."

I should have never told her that part about my parent's savings.

"Look, all I'm saying is that we need to think long and hard about how we want to go about this, babe. I mean, just yesterday my parents wanted to strangle me because we weren't getting married. Do you know what they will do to us — no, do to *me* — when they find out we went ahead and got hitched like a couple of gypsies?

They'll strangle me, hang me, slit my throat, chop out my tongue, filet my skin — and then they'll kill me."

"You're overreacting. I don't think telling our folks we got married is going to be nearly the ordeal you think it will be. If anything, they'll be excited to find out we finally went through with it."

Note: This is the kind of reaction that can only be expressed by a woman whose husband was stupid enough to have his wife meet his mother during Thanksgiving dinner five years prior to the date of their wedding. Only a woman with a husband who is thick enough to provide his wife with as little information about the woman who shat him from her womb could have such a relaxed reaction. Only a man such as the asshole mentioned in this paragraph would go as far as to offer his wife's neck to an aging vampire. My new wife had a lot to learn about being the daughter-in-law of one Clara Abigail O'Sullivan McNulty.

"I know we just got married, and there is a lot we need to figure out now that we have done the equivalent of eloping in Vegas," I said. "But can we just sit here and enjoy our meal as husband and wife without talking about what we need to do i.e. a reception?"

"Sure we can. I just think having a wedding reception would be nice."

June sounded defeated and perplexed, and who could blame her? But I wasn't worried about her feelings at the time. I just wanted the reception conversation to end as soon as was humanly possible.

I nodded my approval, and we sat and finished our pizzas and beer — well, I did, June has a stomach equivalent to a canary's — and talked about her moving in, what furniture she would bring with her and what she would give away. None of this part bothered me. I had been looking forward to it for a long time. I had even cleaned out half of my closet to accommodate her clothes. It was only later that I figured out half of my closet would not hold one quarter of the clothes June decided to bring with her, let alone the clothes she gave away.

The server returned with our check. I told her thank you. I reached for my wallet, deciding I would tip her big for having the common sense to leave us to our food once she brought it to us. But when I felt for my wallet, it wasn't there. It wasn't in any of my pockets.

"What's wrong?" June said.

"My wallet, it's not here."

"Is this how our marriage is going to go? You pretending to forget your wallet?"

"I'm serious. I must have left it at St. Mary's."

"In the confession booth, no doubt. You certainly spent more time in there than you did in bed with me and a bit handsy I have to say."

Now I was a cheapskate *and* a lousy lay? What the fuck is that?

"Babe, do you think you can pay the bill? Then we can go back to St. Mary's to see if my wallet is there?"

"Of course. But I'm telling you right now, this kind of thing will have to stop when we get our joint checking account."

June paid the bill with her credit card, and we left in my car for the church. As we drove over, I thought about June's warning to me and how the fruits of married life were already coming to bear.

God is a spiteful bitch.

TWO

I already felt bad about having sex before I was married, before June and I were married. It didn't matter to me that I lost my virginity to the woman I married; it only mattered that I had lost my virginity *before* I was married. Like I said before, I'm not the kind of guy who takes punishment lightly. So when we arrived at the church I stepped out of the car, feeling my pockets for my rosary and preparing to do another round of Our Fathers and Hail Marys when The Big Guy decided to take my penance a little bit further.

"Is that your mom walking toward us?" June asked.

"What?"

"That's your mother, right?"

"Oh shit."

I don't have to tell you what came next. I mean, I know I do, but you'll understand if I take my sweet time getting to this next part. It's the kind of biblical experience you hear spared-life people talk about — like the guy who was hurled from his motorcycle at breakneck speed onto the hot hard asphalt below, breaking bones and severing muscle tissue only to live in spite of his horrific accident. As if his being crippled for the rest of his life wasn't bad enough, he would have to relive that experience over and over again each time somebody had balls big enough to ask him why he was a paraplegic. It's like the Cherokee Indian you don't hear about. You know — the guy who hunted that black bear in the Ouachita Mountains only to never be heard from again. Is it possible *that* brave Cherokee decided left his people and just kept walking? Of course it is. Is it more likely some black bear — or some other large predatory animal indigenous to Oklahoma — ate his overzealous and colossally stupid ass? I think the answer here also is yes. Better yet? It's like the guy who was the only man to return home from his platoon after being drafted into the Vietnam War. That dude doesn't have to say anything at all for you to understand how he's feeling. His eyes alone can tell you about the carnage his body, his soul witnessed in the Asian jungle. Any man or woman with courage enough to ask a man of war what happened needs to seriously work on their sensitivity skills. In any case, something akin to anyone of the former embarrassments and cruelties to the human psyche could have taken place all because I made the mistake of getting married without my mother in attendance.

Moving at a brisk power walker's pace, my mother was on June and I in a flash from the church parking lot. She was dressed as if she had come straight from Mass — and then it dawned on me that I hadn't attended service. And why wasn't I there? Oh yeah, because I was busy fornicating with my then fiancée just hours before my hours old marriage. So not only had I missed Mass on a Sunday, I had missed Mass on a Sunday to commit an immoral sin during Mass on a Sunday.

Well, this did hurt a little bit.

"This is why you missed Mass, Michael?" my mother said, flailing her arms about in something that was supposed to look like a flowery dress but looked more like hippie wallpaper. She was clearly hysterical, and for the first time in my life, I thought she had a right to be.

"It can't be can it?" my mother said. Her mascara started running due to the tears pouring out of her eyes like water out of an overflowing dam. Fiona used to tell my mother to invest in the waterproof stuff but my mother resisted, claiming that she never became moist around the eyes. Liar, liar, pants on fire.

"Tell me it isn't so, Michael. Tell me you did not commit to the holiest of unions without your mother in a pew to see it done. Tell me it isn't so."

"The hell did I do?"

A swift right hand caught me upside a red thatch of my head.

"Don't you talk like that to me."

I tried to answer her question, but my mother cut me off before I could manage to get another syllable out.

"There I was just getting up from my seat in the pew after hearing a glorious sermon from Father Jacob. Do you know what Father Jacob's sermon was about?" She stopped me before I could answer again. "Of course you don't. You weren't *there*. The sermon was about the merits and rewards of marriage and the honorable way to go about the institution in the eyes of God. You and . . . *her*," she said, pointing her stubby finger at June, "could have learned a thing or two this morning."

"But I was going to make vespers tonight. I swear I—"

My mother popped me upside the head gain with the speed of a Floyd Mayweather Jr. jab. The woman has always had quick hands, and when you take into account I'm every bit of a foot taller than her, you have no choice but to marvel at the speed and fluidity with which she is able to continually strike me. It's something I've never become used to — I have simply learned to endure it.

"After the sermon I went through the procession, like I always do, to pay my respect to Father Jacob and do you know what he tells me?" my mother said. "He tells me congratulations. Yes, he tells me congratulations on my new daughter-in-law and wishes me the best. Now I know that Ron is married because *I* was there. I know that Fiona may be pregnant out of wedlock, but by the grace of God she is not in love with one of those foul lesbian women or a Pentecostal man." I faintly heard June giggle and subtly hip-bumped her in the hope that she would stop before my mother quit her hysterical rambling and caught on. "So that leaves me to ponder the whereabouts and motives of my middle child and most unruly offspring. Now that I have found you, since you have neglected to answer your phone for the entire day, tell me you haven't married this, this *woman* without your mother of all people, who brought you into this world, who fed and clothed you since you were a babe, in attendance at a decent, holy white wedding?"

My mother was out of breath. Her chest heaved and her brow was furrowed. In the time she stopped to confront me, her face had turned from its usual white red-freckled blank canvas to a flaming, pink-flushed Picasso abstraction. Or as my brother would say, she was *pissed* — and not in the drunk Bog-trotter kind of way.

I looked at my mother and then to June, unsure of exactly the best way to approach answering my mother's explosion of terror and parental pain. Dealing with my mother at her most vulnerable was not my strong suit — probably because I hadn't seen her that way but once. And that was the one day my father decided not to return home after she kicked him out of the house for hitting me. He stayed away for a few days, probably shacking up in the office of the mill. When he finally came home, my mother was so happy to have him back that she didn't even ask him where he had been. And what's more? My father got free reign to wail on me whenever he felt the need after that.

I felt June grab my hand and her fingers slowly interlocked with mine. I looked down briefly at our hands, black and white fingers gripping each other with equal might, drawing strength from one another. My mother stood staring at June and I, moving her eyes back and forth between us expectantly.

"Yes, June and I are married, mother," I said proudly. And then I promptly dropped June's hand to go inside St. Mary's to retrieve my lost wallet.

Don't look at the page like that. Don't act surprised. What else did you expect me to do? I was already under a lot of pressure as it was. Besides, June and my mother had never really had that heart-to-heart conversation all girlfriends, fiancées and daughter-in-laws need to have and that was a great opportunity for them to do that — or so I tell myself now. This also is another situation in which my brother would call me a chicken shit. And yet again, I would have to concur with his assessment.

I guess I could have lied to her. I could have told my mother Father Jacob was full of shit and that the woman on my arm was just some floozy I met at the bar last night. It certainly would have sound better to my mother than the alternative. But I couldn't lie to my mother, not about my marriage to June. Besides, Fiona would have told her the truth later anyway. My sister can't hold onto a secret to save her life.

It turns out my wallet was wedged in between the seat and the wall of the confession booth. It had probably slipped out while I was strangling those rosary beads. As I was stepping out of the confessional booth, I saw Father Jacob leaving the sacristy. The church was empty of any remaining good Catholics, and I was in no hurry to return to the intense raging argument I was sure was being contested outside on the church steps between the two most intimidating and strong-willed women I have ever had any intimate connection with. So me being me, I decided to walk over to Father Jacob and strike up a conversation.

"May I speak with you, Father? I need to ask you a question." An arbitrary question most people just ask as a conversation starter, but leave it to my priest to give it his best shot.

"As long as you are not speaking to me from the great world of light that lies behind all human destinies, I think I am still a man who may be able to give you some assistance."

Is your priest able to call up long forgotten quotes from great American poet Henry Wadsworth Longfellow on a whim? Did your priest graduate from the University of Tulsa with degrees — yes, degrees plural — in History, Philosophy and English literature. I didn't think so. He did all that just to one day take a vow of poverty and relinquish all rights to the warm goodness of the female anatomy he might have had. I'm not bragging here so much as I just thought you should know what kind of erudite human being I was dealing with.

"Thank you, Father. May I ask you a personal question?"

"By all means, my son; I have just married you and have received your confession for quite some time now. I think now is as good a time as any to ask me a personal question. Though I do hope it isn't why I took the clerical vow of celibacy. I get that one all the time, though mostly from young men who want to know what to do with their erections."

"What do you do with your erections?"

"Is that the personal question you wish to ask me?"

"Oh, no Father, sorry. The question I mean to ask you is . . . how old are these stained glass windows?" I was stalling and embarrassed. But mostly stalling.

Father Jacob looked me up and down, studying my posture and then settling on my eyes as if he knew something I did not. I wanted to break his gaze, but I couldn't. Father Jacob, much like my best friend James, has a knack for reading me and his wisdom has always proved invaluable for me.

"You know, this marriage business is hard work," Father Jacob said. "You have to want it to want as much as you have ever wanted anything in your life, and then you have to do the work to *make* it work. Most couples these days — over fifty percent of America if you believe the statisticians — don't want to do the work. But I don't believe the statisticians. I believe God. And God has always been one to support the union of man and woman. Do you believe God, Michael?"

This is the part where any good Catholic is *obligated* to say yes.

"Then you have nothing to worry about," Father Jacob said. "I believe you and June are paired perfectly to compliment each other's strengths and compensate for each other's weaknesses, otherwise I would not have given you my blessing. You will see. As this life presents you with obstacles, you will find strength in each other."

"Thank you, Father," I said unsure that this was the wisdom I wanted from him, but I thanked him nonetheless. I shook his hand, genuflected to The Emaciated One above the pulpit and turned to leave when Father Jacob called out to me.

"I'm sure that mother of yours can't wait for you and your new wife to produce some grand kids. I only ask that it be me who christens them."

Grand kids. Plural.

I haven't been married to June for more than few hours and already my priest — of all people — is talking to me about grand kids. How do you react to this? Do you say, "Sure thing. We plan to get to that bit of business tonight"? How come no one prepares you to deal with this question in high school? I could have done a whole lot more with that piece of advice in sex-ed class than the proper way to put on and dispose of a condom. So instead of saying anything at all, I merely shook my head, neither acknowledging nor denying Father Jacob's request, and started to speed walk toward the church exit. First, I couldn't wait to get into the warm blanket of the church and now I couldn't wait to remove myself from its stifling heat. Such is my relationship with The Big Guy.

THREE

With my wallet in hand, I walked out of the empty church asking myself why I had ever thought to seek refuge there. Then I caught sight of my mother and wife and remembered exactly why I had vaulted myself through those great wooden doors in the first place.

As I walked closer to the conversation between two of the three women that consumed my life, I didn't hear what I expected to hear. I expected to hear all matter of racial epithets being hurled without caution. I expected to hear an old battle axe and a young saber dueling fitfully with one another. I expected to hear Jim Lampley, Larry Merchant and Emmanuel Steward calling the bout ringside from St. Mary's steps with Mills Lane in the center of a squared circle soliciting instructions to watch the low blows and the rabbit punches. But I didn't witness any of those things. What I did see was my mother and my new wife getting along famously — Princess Di riding in a parade famously; Sandra Dee in *Imitation of Life* famously. I mean, the way they were talking with each other inspired thoughts of Mayberry — like the worst thing that could happen in life was finding out Andy Taylor's wife was dead and that was the real reason she was never around. It was downright creepy.

Of course, that was what I had hoped would happen all along. But this was too good to be true. I could have sworn I saw something like that in an episode of *The Twilight Zone* once. It didn't end well for the male lead.

At first I thought better of walking toward them but my curiosity quickly overcame rational me, and I had to see if I would merely need to have my eyes checked or book an appointment with nearest shrink.

"Ah, here is my problem child now," my mother said. She took out something that looked like a breath mint and tossed it into her mouth. "You know Michael was the last of my three children to stop wetting the bed. It's true. My oldest, Ronald, quit when he was nine and my youngest, Fiona, quit when she was just four, but Michael, he wet the bed well into his teens. We went through four mattresses with him."

June started laughing with the kind of gusto that would make you think I wasn't physically standing next to her. "He told me he used to wet the bed," June said, "but nothing like what you have just described, Abby."

Abby? Who the fuck is *Abby?* June talked with my mother for twenty minutes and already was on a nickname basis with her?

"Oh heavens yes, Junie. There is no amount of laundry detergent or bleach that can get out a Michael Martin McNulty pee stain."

Junie? What the *fuck?* Clearly, I have missed something — and by something I mean the whole fucking target.

"Martin?" June said, looking at me quizzically.

"My goodness, child. Has my son told you nothing? Michael, there is no reason for you to keep anything from your spouse, least of all your christened name. Shame on you." My mother turned back to June. "I suppose I we really will have to have a girls' night at some point if for no other reason than for me to tell you all about the man you have just married, especially seeing as he has glossed over such details as his middle name."

I hadn't glossed over anything. June was just milking the moment, and I knew it. And girls' night? I didn't even know my mother knew what that term meant.

"Not to mention," my mother continued, "we will have to plan the wedding reception. It won't be as big or brilliant as the wedding we had planned for you, but it will serve as great time for both sides of the family to formally introduce themselves."

"Wait," I said. "We're having a wedding reception? When? With what money?"

"I think it would be nice to have it during the summer," my mother said. "June told me she had already spoken with you about it earlier this morning. And don't worry, the same suckers who spent thousands of dollars on a wedding that didn't happen yesterday will be prepared to fit the bill."

"But ma—"

"Don't you 'But ma' me, mister. You have deprived me of my right as your mother to see you married off to this fine young woman. You will not deprive me of a wedding reception. Now suck it up and make your mother happy, or come Hell or high water I will tan your hide redder than a summer tomato."

My mother had issued a command to her middle child, and as such, it was to be followed without question. A Southern Baptist man would have simply told his mother to shove it and went on with his unseemly marriage. But me? I'm a sucker for a good guilt trip. How very Catholic of me.

My mother bid us goodbye and walked off much more chipper than she came. I stood next to June watching my mother leave, trying to wait for my mother to drive off before I asked her what the hell just happened.

"Your mother is a nice lady," June said. "I can't believe it has taken you this long to introduce her to me."

"Don't be fooled. *That* was not my mother. She is an alien — a pod person from the planet Vulcan. My mother is . . . different." I couldn't bring myself to tell June about the meaner, nastier side of my mother that I had grown to know all too well over the course of my childhood. After all, people change in one day all the time, right?

"You're being silly. But at least we are going to have the wedding reception I wanted."

Keywords: I wanted. Not *we wanted* but *I wanted.*

"Come on, we need to go by my apartment and pick up a few things, and we'll need to get me a key made to your apartment and that furniture you have — or should I say those bean bags — will have to go, sweetheart."

"The Spartans weren't big on furniture."

"But a legendary Greek warrior, you are not. And those posters of those rap stars you love so much will have to go. They're hideous."

This is the part where I reminded myself of the things this woman did for me, of the shit she puts up with from me. Besides, isn't compromise what marriage is all about, what love is about?

Some Months Later

FOUR

I woke up early to get to work at the Norman Sentinel. For some reason, I wanted to leave my apartment as quickly as possible. I just felt uncomfortable. It wasn't too hot or extremely cold, yet I felt stifled from the moment I awoke in bed next to June.

On the drive to work, I stopped at the Brown Stain closest to my building to pick up my first cup of coffee. The essence of the coffee bean has become a necessity for me since first being hired on at the Sentinel. Deadlines, interviews, fact-checking and word counts have left me with little sleep and less energy. Like the fish needs water, the reporter needs gallons of coffee. No doubt Brown Stain has made its entire fortune over-selling its product to journalists because, like crack fiends in need of a fix, we don't care how much it costs as long as it gets into the blood stream.

When I strutted into the little shop off the corner of Asp and Boyd, I found there was no line whatsoever. I think that was a first. Even on Sunday mornings there were at least four people standing in front of the cash register.

The barista at the register was a younger-looking man who stood just over six feet with long, grungy brown hair. His body language said he didn't want to be there. I wanted to tell him the grunge look went out when Kurt Cobain took a 20-gauge to his noggin, but I resisted the urge. I didn't want to taste a thin filmy pump of extra mucus I had once before after insisting that listening to Nickelback was a form of masochism.

"Order something," the barista said.

Not the most promising opening line from a fast food cashier, but I needed coffee and was willing to overlook it. "Just a tall Bold Pick of the Day."

"You get that every day."

"I know."

"How about you try something different?"

"The Bold Pick of the Day is something different every day, isn't it?"

"Not every day."

"Then why call it the Bold Pick of the Day?"

"Because marketing won't let us call it, Whatever The Fuck I Want to Give You That's Brewed And Still Lukewarm."

"So you're telling me you don't brew me something different each time I ask for the Bold Pick of the Day?"

"That's what I'm telling you."

"That's disheartening."

"Tragic stuff, I know."

"Why reveal this astounding revelation to me?"

"Because I pity you."

"You pity me? Why should you pity me?"

"You're a corporate underling who's given up."

"No, I'm not."

"Look man, you don't have to lie to me. I see dudes like you every day."

"Like me?"

"Sure. Dudes like you come in here every morning in your two piece suits, pressed white shirts, brass cuff links and buffed wingtips. You come in here looking defeated. You've given up on your dream for a cubicle, a computer and a TPS report."

"What dream have I given up on?"

"Shit, I don't know. Maybe you wanted to paint. You know Hitler wanted to paint and his pops told him no and just like that there were two world wars because some idiot dad wouldn't let his kid paint rainbows and shit. He should've let him paint, man. Or maybe you wanted to be a writer. Writers are known for jumping off bridges, sticking their heads in ovens and shit."

"What makes you think I am not living my dream right now?"

"Because just a few months ago when you let me charge you four bucks for a cup of coffee you could've got for fifty cents at McDonalds you didn't have that piece of gold wrapped around your finger. Now you wear that thing daily, but with such utter fucking disdain — like you're some kind of Vietnam vet who kept that piece of shrapnel in his ass to remind you of fallen bros or something. You've not only given up, bro — you've given in. You're a dream quitter just like the rest of 'em."

"Look, I'd love to stand here and chat with you about life and living the dream as you no doubt are, but could you please just make my lukewarm over-priced coffee? I need to get to work."

"No."

"No? What do you mean, *no?*"

"I mean no. I'm not going to make another decision for you, dream quitter. Your squeeze may have your nuts in a vice but I don't see her lurking around here, so that means you're free to make a decision on your own."

"I make plenty of my own decisions."

"Prove it. Make one right now, dream quitter," the barista said, pointing to the Brown Stain menu behind him.

"I want the Bold Pick of the Day."

"Fine," he said, exasperatedly. The barista walked away from the counter, picked up a Brown Stain paper cup, walked to the sink and filled the cup with water. He put a lid over it and handed it to me.

"What is that?" I said.

"Bold Pick of the Day."

"All right, enough of this shit. I want to speak to the manager."

"I'm listening," he said, leaning over the counter.

"I asked to speak to the manager."

"And I said I'm listening."

I looked at him ponderously, and then he pointed to his name tag: Steve, manager. Fuck. "I guess I'll have something different today."

"That's the way, dream quitter."

"What do you suggest?"

"Have you learned nothing?"

Eventually, I walked out of Brown Stain with a tall, non-fat caffé mocha with whipped cream and three pumps of caramel, two pumps of hazelnut and five of peppermint cream not knowing exactly what kind of concoction I had just created. But one thing was certain: It was my creation and that was all that mattered to the Brown Stain barista-manager-Kurt-Cobain-clone named Steve. During the drive to the Sentinel, I actually started thinking about what he said about me giving up on my dream and not being able to make a decision. But I wasn't able to dwell on it for too long after I looked down at my watch. I was going to be late for the morning desk meeting.

FIVE

The Norman Sentinel is the kind of place a person with O.C.D. might lose their mind in. The word unorganized does not even begin to cover it. The newsroom is littered with Styrofoam and paper coffee cups, left over newspapers — we buy them off the stands in the hopes that we might keep our jobs in this new paperless economy — and a constant, constipated buzzing feels the air with a kind of white noise you learn to ignore after a few weeks. That or you go insane from the sheer chaos of it all.

I ran through the doors hoping to make it back to the conference room before the meeting was over while trying to think up some lame excuse I could give to my testy, over-worked and paranoid boss Larry Bransetter. Larry is a nice enough guy once you're able to convince him you are not the twenty-something newbie who the editor-in-chief and publisher of the Sentinel are grooming to take over his job.

About the same time I was "promoted" to the sports desk, Larry was demoted as managing editor. It turns out Larry was one of those guys who had a talent for burning out reporters quicker than a ten cent candle. Rather than deal with the constant complaints of beaten down reporters or going through the hassle of firing Larry, the editor-in-chief at the Sentinel, Merlin Ellis, thought it best to give Larry a breather — so he made him the sports editor.

The truth is no one in their right mind wants to be the sports editor at the Sentinel. The pay sucks, the hours are ridiculous and deadlines are always stacked against you. And that's even if the reporters on the desk emailed him their copy on time. Larry's section is the first one most Norman denizens turn to and it had better be correct, or he would here about. How would you like not just your boss but the customers telling you how bad you are at your job on a daily basis? Yeah, me neither.

"McNulty, you're thirty minutes late," Larry said as I tried to sneak into the room surreptitiously.

"Sorry, Larry. I got caught in—"

"Never mind what you were doing. Just sit down and shut up."

"All right, people. Chief Ellis wants more features and more hard news," Larry said from the head of the fake-oak boardroom table.

I always thought it was tragic the way Larry addressed the three reporters he had on the desk. He stood at the end of the table with both hands planted on it, beads of sweat emanating from his brow, talking at a volume that was loud enough for the entire newsroom to hear him through the conference room's glass window. It wasn't as if he was editing The New York Times' sports section, but don't try telling Larry that.

"We need to write investigative pieces," Larry said. "We need to do the kind of investigative journalism that would have those Pulitzer pricks begging to hand us that goddamn award."

"But Larry we write sports," I said.

"You're damn right we do, McNulty, and that's where the action is in this town. Norman is ripe with corruption. I'll bet those athletic department pricks at OU are paying players under the table and bribing officials as we speak. And we need the story. We need sources on the inside of the Crimson and White Cartel. And to illustrate to each of you how serious I am I'm giving the assistant sports editor job to the reporter in this room who can bring me the goods."

Oh yeah, Larry, all of us can't wait to be the middle man between you and the rest of us. So, not only can we shovel your shit, but we'll become the bane of our colleagues' existence too. Gee, thanks.

"Now, get out there and bring me some human interest stories, some ground-breaking, boots-on-the-ground journalism," Larry said.

It was right at that moment that I sincerely thought about applying for the gossip columnist job.

After leaving the meeting, I had planned to go to my cubicle and tidy up a bit, but that plan was stopped when Marty Anderson decided to drop by and plopped his ass on top of my desk. A heavy-set man and another lifer at the Sentinel, Marty is one of those sleazy know-it-alls on the news desk. The problem with guys like Marty isn't that there know-it-alls or even that they're sleazy — those two traits combined make for a damn good reporter — it's that he's a bitter, sleazy, know-it-all who sweats like an altar boy at a peep show. I had to disinfect my desk later.

"Hey, I heard you got married, McNulty," Marty said.

"Yeah, Marty, I did . . . a few months ago."

"You know Nora and I have been married for sixteen years, McNulty. That's nine away from the big silver anniversary."

He said that like it should've meant something to me. It didn't then, and it doesn't now.

"You know why it's lasted so long?" he said.

I shook my head.

"We did it right. We didn't get married until we were in our thirties, not like you kids today who get married straight out of college like it's part of the graduation ceremony. You see, we both had our fun before we even met each other. I can't tell you how many women I bagged before I met Nora, and the truth of it is, before I met her I was at the clinic quite a bit. The gals couldn't get enough of Little Marty. There was one woman by the name of Lela. Boy, I tell you the night I finally got her in the sack—"

Oh, Jesus Christ, make it stop. Make it stop right now.

"You know what? That's not important."

Oh, thank *God*. Thank you, sweet baby Jesus.

"What is important is that we were both ready to be married. And when we decided we were both ready we were respectful enough to inform our parents — to have a nice, respectable white wedding with our friends and family in attendance."

"I'm sure your folks were quite happy with you, Marty."

I turned toward my computer in an effort to start writing the three hundred word advance I needed to file for tomorrow night's Stark High basketball game, but Marty wouldn't take my subtle hint. He just kept right on talking.

"They were, and I can't imagine what they might have said or done to me if Nora and I had done what I heard you and your new wife have done. I heard it was a shotgun wedding. I heard it was the kind of wedding that only happens in Vegas. I heard you didn't even know your witnesses."

"You hear a lot."

"I'm a reporter, buddy. That's my job."

"So you've told me many times before."

"Anyway, I wanted to congratulate you and welcome you to Hell on Earth. We've always got room for one more."

"How kind of you."

"You know any other man would be a little depressed about the prospect of bedding just one woman for the rest of his life, but not you McNulty. You're taking it in stride. I like that about you."

"Thanks, Marty. I think."

"No, really. You're just the kind of guy a woman looks for when she starts to get starry-eyed about the idea of getting hitched. You're the kind of guy that gives the rest of us a bad name." Marty was starting to ooze. I could see the pit stains growing larger, seeping through his white dress shirt.

"What makes you say that?" I said.

"You're still trainable."

"Trainable?"

"Trainable — like a newborn puppy or circus animal. You see, women, they love a trainable man. They want a man who hasn't sown his oats all over, that hasn't come anywhere near good pussy or, in your case, a vagina at all. They want a guy who gets so excited at the thought of fucking at all that he'll allow a woman to train him to do it the way she wants — the way she *likes* it. And that's what you are, McNulty. You're trainable."

"Is this supposed to be a pep talk, Marty?"

"Hey man, I'm just trying to clue you in on why a woman would first say no and then say yes to a marriage proposal inside of a seventy-two-hour window."

"How did you—"

"I'm a reporter, McNulty. That's my job. My advice: Divorce her before this marriage blows up in your just-popped-cherry face. She doesn't want you. She wants a steady line of cash and a man who believes the sun rises and sets on her ass."

Before I could rebut Marty patted me on the shoulder with one of his clammy hands and walked away. Surely he was going to spread the good news of marriage to another wayward soul.

I reached into my desk drawer to pull out my AP Style book, put on a set of headphones and opened the iTunes program on my computer's desktop. Just as I jacked my headphones into my computer, Ellis' secretary, Greta Jenkins, tapped me on the shoulder.

"Mr. Ellis wants to see you in his office."

"Really? What does he want with a lowly sportswriter like me?"

"I don't ask questions, Mr. McNulty. I simply follow orders."

And Marty says *I'm* trained.

"Sure thing," I said. "I'll be in there as soon as I file my copy."

"No. You misunderstand me. He wants to see you *now*."

"Right now?"

"Yes, Mr. McNulty, right now."

I followed Greta through the maze of desks and newspaper folk into a long corridor that led to one singular destination. Greta's desk was just outside the corridor and acted as the one entrance in and out of Ellis' office. I felt like Mad Max just before he was thrown into the Thunderdome.

"Hey, Greta," I said, "you'd warn me if I was about to get fired? I mean, you wouldn't send me in there like a horse at a glue factory, right?"

Greta pointed down the hallway. "He's expecting you."

I walked down the hallway with my right hand in my pocket, pinching the hell out of my rosary beads.

I had only seen the inside of Merlin Ellis' office once. That day was the day after I was hired to write at the paper; the day the sweet scantily clad woman from human resources was fired. I think it was a coincidence. At least, I hope it a coincidence. I never screwed up the courage to ask anyone where she had gone or what she had done to get fired. All I knew was that there was a new HR person — a man this time — who was going to settle into her office. I wrote that to write this: The less you know around the Sentinel the better. Hence the reason I have never bothered to know or be known by Chief Ellis.

Ellis is rumored to have a Geronimo quote mounted behind and above his desk and is said to be the kind of man who takes pride in firing folks. He doesn't farm it out to any of his section editors, and I know he doesn't ask the HR dude to do it because that dude sits on his ass doing less than nothing all day — a killer job if you ask me. No, if you were going to get let go, terminated, put out to pasture or just plain whacked, Chief Ellis was going to perform the scalping. You have to respect — and fear, Oh God yes, you must fear — a man like that. I suddenly wished Ellis' moniker had more to do with his being editor-in-chief of the Sentinel and less to do with his similarities to a man who once had "The Terrible" tacked onto the end of his first name.

Walking into Ellis' office, I felt like a lone Calvary officer who was about to get his scalp well and truly peeled and dried in the wicked heat of the sun and nailed to the nearest totem pole. I knocked on the door and heard a gruff grunt come from behind the wide oak frame. I assumed the guttural sound meant for me to enter, which is probably why I stayed my white ass put.

"Get in here, McNulty," I heard from behind the door.

I slowly opened the door and found the chief sitting in a large leather chair. He was a short man, but his shoulders and chest bulged through his blue dress shirt and red tie. He wore red suspenders and was fidgeting with them when I stepped into his office.

"How are you?" Chief Ellis asked.

It was an arbitrary question, but I thought it best not to blow it off.

"I'm good, sir. I love my job, sir." I needed to add that. We all need to add that little piece of assurance for our superiors and this is especially true for us who do actually love our jobs.

"Good, good," Chief Ellis said. "How is everything on the sports desk?"

"It's good, sir." If I don't say too much, there is less chance of me saying too much. Get me?

"Yeah, Larry is a bit off, I know, but he means well."

"Yes, sir. I know he does. He's a good boss, and I like working under him."

Well, there is one lie I'll be in confessing to Father Jacob.

"Really? I always thought Larry was a little too over bearing on his staff, but he's an excellent line editor all the same. And you fellas over in sports seem to draw a good bead on your beats. Especially you, McNulty. So I thought sports would be a good move for him. He can't do too much harm there. Am I right?"

"Yes sir. You are right."

Blessed me Father for I have sinned. Again.

Chief Ellis placed both elbows on his desk, bathing me in wrinkled forehead focus and said, "How do you think the sports desk would be without you?"

"Sir?"

"You know, how good do you think the sports section would be without your byline?"

This is a loaded question, which means there is a hollow point in each chamber, and the chief has effectively wrapped my hand around the grip, placed my finger on the trigger and pointed the barrel at my temple. If I told him how great the other writers are on the desk and how outside of OU sports and the Norman high schools there wasn't much to write, then I'd be talking myself out of my job. If I told him how great I thought I was at my job and continued to talk about how I'm the only person on the desk who has never missed a deadline, then I'd sound like an asshole and a prima donna. See, loaded question.

"Well sir, I—" was stalling for time. Rarely do words escape me. I'm a writer. It's my job to produce words others cannot, especially when others are speechless. But this time it wasn't that words didn't come to mind, they just weren't the right words.

"Before you answer, let me tell you about this quote above my desk," he said.

Oh, thank you, God. Thank you so much for bailing me out.

"Have you seen this quote before?"

Dude, I was blinded by my own stupidity just a moment ago. I would not have seen Nina Hartley naked if she was four feet in front of me. By all means keep talking.

"I'll read it to you. It says, 'I was no chief and never had been, but because I had been more deeply wronged than others, this honor was conferred upon me, and I resolved to prove worthy of the trust.' Do you know who said that?"

Not the slightest fucking clue.

"The great Apache warrior-chief Geronimo said that. He was speaking about the honor and responsibility of being named chief of his people."

Okay, this took the whole Chief Ellis thing to an entirely different level.

"I can sympathize with the man," Chief Ellis said. "Did you know I started out writing sports just like you?"

"No sir, I didn't."

To be fair, there is less paper on Merlin Ellis and his achievements than James Bond. The only things you will find of his are a few bylines from his early writing career in the Sixties. But since the late Seventies the man has been editing the Sentinel. In Norman, this makes him slightly more mysterious than Gandalf the Grey and more powerful than Sauron could have ever hoped to have been.

"I never liked writing sports, you understand," Chief Ellis said, "but what's a junior reporter to do?"

I shrugged my shoulders. I could sympathize.

"Anyway, the reason I brought you in here is to ask you to move from the high school sports beat to writing news features?"

Well, that was unexpected. "What?" I said.

"I want you to be my new feature writer."

"You mean you're not going to can me?" That's as eloquent as I could be under the circumstances. Sue me.

"*Can* you? No, son, I'm not going to can you. The truth is you being a married man and all now has sealed it for me. You're one the best writers I've got and the fact is Myron Goodson is retiring at the end of the month and I want this job to go to a man I trust and who has some experience at the Sentinel."

The mind is blank. The body is numb. Only my utter stupidity remains.

"Do you want the position or not?" he said.

"Sure."

That's all I could come up with on a three-second deadline. Sue me.

"Good, good. Greta will fill you in on the particulars. But I will go ahead and tell you I need you to start this next week. That means you'll need to talk to Marty Anderson and see what he's looking for out of you."

Ah shit. I forgot about Marty. "Yes sir, thank you sir," I said.

"Don't thank me now. Thank me by producing quality features."

I turned to walk out of the door and heard Chief Ellis call my name. "Do this right, McNulty. I don't want to have to can you." He smiled and chuckled at his statement. I did not.

SIX

At her desk, Greta informed me the promotion would come with a hefty ten thousand dollar raise. Even today that is a lot of money — especially when you take into account that raise made up roughly half of my meager earnings for the year. I live in a city where rent is still comparatively cheap, and yet I only made enough at this job to afford a one bedroom studio apartment that came with rather large and brazen cockroaches for roommates. At first, the relationship between me and my six-legged friends was scary and odd, but we have since learned to adapt to each other's peculiar and gross weirdness. This means that I stay out of the kitchen for the most part. I eat a lot of take out.

Greta handed me my new contract with my responsibilities as feature writer placed on top. She wanted to be sure I knew what I was getting myself into.

"You should know that Mr. Ellis doesn't usually give such jobs to men as . . . young as you are."

You would be wise to replace "young" in Greta's sentence with "inexperienced," or even "unproven." I did.

"And from the sports desk," Greta said. "One would think Mr. Ellis would have promoted someone who has actual experience reporting news."

"I'll try not to let him down."

"I should hope not. Mr. Ellis is usually such a good judge of talent and character."

Ouch.

I tried to walk away, thinking with the forms and contract in my hand that this was a win no matter how scathing Greta's comments were. I mean, I was the one walking away from Chief Ellis' office not only with my scalp still well and truly attached to my skull but with a thirty-three percent pay raise.

"You know most men would have had the good sense to respect the natural way of things. Most men understand that some things just don't mix no matter how you combine the ingredients, but not you, Mr. McNulty. You seem hell bent on race mixing."

This should be the part where I stand up for my wife and the love of my life. This should be the part where I tell Greta how ass-backward her thinking is. This should be the part where I inform her that this is the twenty-first century and Americans don't think that way anymore. This should be the part where I tell Greta how disappointed and angry I am with her for her close-minded attitude. This should be the part where Martin Luther King Jr.'s words and sentiments should tumble out of me like the rushing tide of the Mississippi River.

But that part didn't happen.

"I will try to do better next time," I said and walked back to my desk.

Try to do better next time? What the fuck does that even mean? Marriage isn't the kind of thing that should require a next time. It's one of the few things in life I'm fairly sure you should try to get right the first time. And try what better? What was I going to get better at? Sure I would have wanted the marriage to have happened as I envisioned; with June's and my family in attendance and the whole nine. But I couldn't have loved June anymore than I already did. I couldn't illustrate that better than I already had — by committing to her "til death do us part" as the vows go.

I'm not going to lie to you. When I got back to my desk, my head was all kinds of fucked up from that conversation with Greta, and the fact that I just received a promotion and pay raise had completely left my conscious mind until I saw a picture of June on my desk. That was what I needed. I needed June's reassurance that everything was going to be all right. But when I reached for my cell phone I smelled funky fumes that only one man — in his infinite furriness — could fester.

"So, McNulty. I hear you're my new feature reporter," Marty said. He leaned over the top of me while I sat helpless in my ergonomically incorrect chair. I found myself reaching for my rosary beads once again, this time praying that no Marty juice would find its way onto any part of my person, but as he inched closer I began to think praying was less and less helpful.

"I just learned that myself," I said.

"Did he read you his quote from that one injun he likes so much?"

"He did."

"I tell you, it makes my blood boil to see a white man revere an injun so much. But not you, huh, McNulty — you're an ardent fan of the dark races."

"Is there something you want from me, Marty?"

"Hey, can't we just have a friendly conversation?"

No, you racist prick. We can't.

"Sure, Marty, it's just I have to finish this advance for the website by five."

"Well I'm sure you can bust that out in a half-hour or so. You're the wordy, fast-typing, wiz kid around here."

A pained look crept across my face.

"Look, McNulty, you weren't my first choice for this job. I was the first to know Myron was retiring, and I spent the last six months trying to convince the chief to let me bring in some new blood for this job. But for some reason he seemed hell-bent on promoting from within the paper. If I had known he was going to completely cut me out of the hiring decision for the most important reporter on my desk and then leave me with a Mick like you, I would have tried harder. But here we are."

Marty leaned in closer to me. I could see the rotting yellow of his teeth.

"I don't care what promises the chief told you in his office," Marty said. "I don't care what kind of arrangement you made with him to get this job. And I don't care what kind of writing you had aspirations of doing. You work for me, on my desk, and your byline will appear in my section only because I put it there. You will write what I tell you to write, how I tell you to write it. There will be none of those flowery adjectives and adverbs you write so much in Larry's section. I want my section as dry as your mother's snatch." Marty leaned back, still holding my gaze. "Now you can write your little advance, McNulty."

I thought about calling June, but I had lost the good feeling I had after leaving Chief Ellis' office. Besides, I don't believe June — or any woman for that matter — wants to hear from her significant other that he is thinking of pulling a David Foster Wallace, and it's probably not a good idea to come home early today.

There's nothing like a successful one-on-one meeting with your new boss. God is a spiteful bitch.

Stark High was scheduled to play Booker T. Washington High in the second round of the state tournament. Tipoff for the boys' game was at 6:05 p.m., but I always made a point of arriving at the gymnasium early enough to catch the JV boys' game and sit through some of the girls' game whenever possible. After I'd written my advance, I decided to go back to Brown Stain — for my second crack fix of the day — and study the roster and stat sheets of Norman and BTW before making my way out to Yukon High for the game. Brown Stain was a little more crowded than it was earlier, but it wasn't full. At the counter, I was greeted by Steve the Judgmental Barista once again.

"What do you say, dream quitter? Come for another lesson in how to make choices?"

"I just came for a cup coffee and a quiet spot to read."

"We've got all kinds of coffee, so you'll have to be more specific than that, dream quitter. And as for a quiet space to read, well, this is about the most rambunctious coffee shop I've ever been associated with. We play music all the time, people are always talking loud and that espresso machine makes an awful racket. Maybe you want to take your coffee outside? It's probably quieter there."

"Rambunctious? That's a big word you used there."

"Fuck you, dream quitter. I have an English degree from that very university across Boyd Street. Fuck publishers if they don't want to read and distribute the truth."

"You went to OU?"

"And you went to the University of Sell Outs and Dream Quitters, didn't you, dream quitter?"

"I'm sorry I just thought—"

"You just thought I was some punk who's a lifer at this coffee shop. Well, I'm not. I haven't given up on my dream like you dream quitter. I'm the next Hemingway, the next Joyce, the next Faulkner all rolled into one. *The Corrections* has nothing on what I'm about to drop on all you pedestrian, dream quitting pseudo-utopian denizens of this slowly degrading society."

"I'm writing a novel too."

"Order your fucking Bold Pick of the Day, man, so I can get on with the business of shilling the coffee bean — A.K.A. legalized crack — to the masses. You disgust me."

"I don't want the Bold Pick of the Day."

"Oh? Have you grown a set of balls in the last few hours? That must be some kind of record."

"I'll have whatever I had this morning."

"Look man, I don't remember all forty-six ingredients I threw in your caffeine cocktail. So this time I'm going to let you go with something that's on the menu."

"Fair enough. I'll have a caffé mocha."

"Hot or cold?"

"Lukewarm."

"Don't be a smartass."

"Hot."

"Okay. Stand over there and I'll call you when your order's ready."

I found a vacant table and sat my bag down next to the side of my chair and pulled out my notes on BTW and Norman to familiarize myself with the teams again. It didn't take me long to figure out who and what to watch for. My notes for BTW read like the '86 Celtics: They were a complete team. Each man knew his job and executed it well. My Stark High notes read nothing like BTW.

I'd been following the Stark High team since I was first put on the desk. I dabbled in writing about OU sports and even covered a couple of Thunder games, but I have acted as the go-to reporter for all things Stark High sports from the beginning. It took some getting used to — beat writing I mean — but I came to enjoy it. I saw the side of players and coaches that is usually reserved for close friends and family. I saw these kids interact with each other in a way that made them human and not the basketball gods they were on the hardwood. Stark High was undefeated at 28-0. All twelve kids on the team were athletic specimens and gifted with the kind of playground talent filmmakers make into documentaries. But one kid was a cut above the rest. His name was Anthony Stallings.

Anthony is one of those prodigious basketball kids we seem to read about with increasing regularity. You know, the kid who is destined to become the next, LeBron James, the next Kobe Bryant, the next Blake Griffin. Anthony ran with the athletic grace of a gazelle and handled the basketball as if it were just an extension of his two hands. Even in Norman, Oklahoma where football is king, Anthony garnered a crowd even in local pick-up games. And why not? At six-foot-eight and weighing just a shade over two hundred and fifty pounds, Anthony is already an imposing physical specimen. Seriously, there are legs attached where his arms should be and thick, oak tree trunks where his legs should be. I wrote a story about him in which one of OU's assistant football coaches said they would extend him a scholarship on athleticism alone, even knowing he had never played a down of organized football in his life. We should all be so physically and athletically fortunate. When I first laid eyes on him at the Stark High gymnasium, he was alone in the gym shooting free throws. Anthony was drenched in sweat; his shirt wet against his body. Really it was by sheer chance I showed up to see Anthony when I did.

I had just got on at the Sentinel and was given some bad information by the sports editor before Larry was bequeathed the job by Chief Ellis. Anyway because I arrived late, I wasn't able to introduce myself to the head coach, let alone get quotes from him and his players for a story I had two hours to write and file once I arrived at the gym. I thought about leaving, thinking I could write my story without quotes and then it struck me how dumb that would be. I was about to call my editor and inform him of my situation when I saw Anthony take off flying through the air, turn three hundred and sixty degrees around and slam home a thunderous dunk with two hands. Call it journalistic intuition or just plain intrigue, but after I saw Anthony do that I knew what I was going to put in my story. My story was only four hundred and fifty words, but the interview — casual conversation, really — I had with Anthony changed my journalism career and the way I cover sports. From then on, I was able to look past just what was happening in the game and able to see through to the people that made the game happen.

"Caffé Mocha for the dream quitter," I heard.

I packed up my belongings, picked up my coffee from the counter and walked back to my car. Interstate-35 north traffic and a gym full of crazed high school basketball fans beckoned. God help me.

SEVEN

The varsity girls' game was just starting the third quarter of play. This gave me time to set up in the stands a few minutes before proceeding to press table where I would have to do my duty. I liked talking with the fans. Too often they know more than sports writers give them credit. Don't get me wrong. There are some yahoos out there, but those pricks travel in drunken packs. The people I like talking with are the mothers and siblings of the kids on the hardwood.

I took a seat in the seventh row on the home side next to a woman wearing the purple and red of the Stark High Dragons — a Dragon Mom. She had a button on her shirt depicting a picture of high school-age girl in a Stark High basketball uniform. I put two and two together and watched Dragon Mom for awhile. After I got a feel for how intensely she was watching the game, I asked her my usual opening question.

"How is she doing?"

"We've worked on this for years and she still doesn't get it," Dragon Mom said, shooting lasers at her daughter's head while she ran up and down the court. "It's all riding on the line, right here. Right now. And she just doesn't *get* it."

"What doesn't she get?"

"Ah, look at her! She's fouling my kid every time she drives the lane. I'm sorry what did you say?"

"What doesn't she get?"

"She doesn't get where she is, the opportunity. She's pissing away all that I have sacrificed and worked for to get her here."

I observed Dragon Mom awhile longer, paying little attention to the game and final score before proceeding to the press table for the boys' game I was there to cover. At the press table, my colleagues had already set up shop. I walked behind the table, which served as the scorer's workspace as well, tipping my hat to the usual suspects. Clive Mills and Bob Cook sat near center of the table, straddling the 8x11.5 laminated placard that had my name typed across it in intimidating capital letters.

"Howdy gents," I said.

"McNulty," Bob said. Bob didn't look up from his work. He was going through his routine of making his homemade stat sheet to keep track of points, fouls, rebounds, steals, blocks and turnovers — otherwise known as The Chart. On The Chart, Bob drew columns using a pencil and ruler on a piece of loose-leaf, notebook paper and labeled each column accordingly. When I first met Bob, I thought he was just another ultra-obsessive reporter who didn't know what to do with himself while the game was going on. It was only after the next day when I read his gamer that I realized just how good he was at his job, and how much better I would need to be at mine if I wanted to keep up. Even Larry took notice of the Bob's work calling it, "a work of art on deadline" and mine, "a piece of shit that my 7-year-old daughter could have written in magenta crayon." To make me feel better Larry added that he was considering sending his 7-year-old in my stead to the next game, saying at least he could "pay her in candy and Barbie dolls." From then on, I mimicked Bob. Yes, I have made The Chart since that day for every game I have ever covered, be it middle school or Division-1A. Sue me.

"How are you, Mikey?" Clive said.

"I'm good, Clive," I said. "You know, just another day at the office."

Well no, it wasn't. But I wasn't going to tell Clive that. Clive is a great sports writer in his own right, like Bob, but his style is considerably different. The guy doesn't take many notes on paper, but he tweets a lot. He is worse than I am at picking up the subtle nuances of the game, but he asks some of the best questions at press conferences. Bob's merit lies in his ability to communicate. He can get people to tell him anything. I remember once telling him he missed his calling as an FBI negotiator. His response: It was too easy a gig.

The starters for each team had been announced by the time I had fully set up my laptop. With the game underway, I thought that was where the action would be, at least for the next two hours. I was wrong.

Midway through the first quarter Clive felt like chatting. "So, Mikey, how's that marriage treating you?"

"It's good."

"I'm glad it's good for you now. The last thing in the world you want is for that ring to morph into a ball and chain, right?"

"Yep, it's good."

I wondered how many ways we could both make the word good mean something totally different than the Oxford English Dictionary definition.

"You know, there may come a time when your marriage isn't good," Clive said. "You know my marriage to Miriam was good right up until the day it got bad. You know when that day was?"

"Nope," I said.

"The day Miriam told me she was pregnant with Hailey."

"No sex?"

"No, that wasn't it, although I don't think that would be too big of deal for a previously celibate fella like you. No, it got bad because a kid in the house changes everything."

"Didn't you and your wife talk about it before getting pregnant?"

"How could we?" Clive said. "She was pregnant less than a year into the marriage. I always thought I wanted kids, but you never know for sure until the doc thrusts a baby into your hands and calls you dad. I didn't want to be a dad. Do you?"

"Sure, I guess."

"You guess? Let me tell you something, Mikey. It would be a crime for anybody to bring a child into this world the way it is now. Hell, I think they should sterilize the lot of us just so we can't inflict our ideals, our environment and our demons on the innocent. You know what I mean?"

"Yeah, I know what you mean."

I didn't say anything more. I couldn't.

The Stark High Dragons defeated the Booker T. Washington Hornets 83-76 in a game that was a lot closer on the scoreboard than if you watched it live — and I had. Anthony Stallings led Stark High in all offensive categories scoring 37 points, dishing out 12 assists and pulling down 16 boards with seven blocks.

Most of the team huddled around their coach and celebrated, but I didn't see the high school phenom in the celebration. I looked around the gym and saw Anthony standing in a corner. A young woman about his age handed him a beautiful baby girl. The baby had brown wavy hair and a tan skin complexion. I decided not to go straight to the press conference area to wait for the players and coaches. Instead, I walked over to Anthony to see if I could get quotes.

"Great game, Anthony."

"Thanks, Mr. McNulty. Are you looking for some quotes?"

"If you don't mind."

"Give me a second to celebrate with my baby girl here."

The words hit me like a ton of bricks falling from the fifty-second floor of the Chrysler Building. "Baby girl?"

"Yeah," Anthony said with a look of surprise on his face. "Oh, you haven't met Michaela have you?" Anthony said, gesturing to his daughter. "Sorry, she's a little tired. It's past her bedtime."

"Hi," I said to Michaela, feebly attempting not to act astonished. "Michaela, huh?"

"Yeah, like the archangel," Anthony said. "We figured he would be more inclined to watch over Michaela when neither of us is looking if we named her after him."

"We?"

"Me and my girlfriend Megan," Anthony said. He pointed with his free hand to the small pale woman standing next to him.

160

"It's nice to meet you," Megan said.

I shook her hand and reciprocated the greeting.

"You looked surprised," Anthony said to me.

"Forgive me, but I *am* a little surprised."

"You shouldn't be," Anthony said. "I knew I liked you that day in the gym, but after I heard you got married to a black woman, well, that's cool, Mr. McNulty. Real cool. Why do you think you're always the first person I call when I have news? Or why do you think I answer your questions and consent to interviews with you when I tell everyone else no?"

It never donned on me that a player — high school kid — gave me preferential treatment. "I guess I figured you thought I was harmless," I said.

"Man, nobody in your line of work is harmless. But like I said, I had a good feeling about you and Megan thinks you're all right."

Megan nodded, agreeing with her boyfriend.

"Hey, Mr. McNulty, let me say goodnight to my baby girl and we can do one of those private interviews," Anthony said.

I watched as this high school basketball star kissed his two ladies good night. For many, such a sight would turn stomachs or, at the very least, make some people feel ridiculously uncomfortable. Me? I was comforted. There were more like me and June. There were more like us.

After the interview was done and my gamer was filed, I headed home to my apartment and wife. When I opened the door June was sitting on the couch in our living room. Her knees were folded up on the cushion and she was holding a mug with two hands.

"I made a pot," June said. "You should probably pour yourself a cup. There's something I need to tell you."

"Oh, okay," I said. "There are some things I need to tell you to — good things."

June didn't smile or nod. She didn't even look up at me. I walked everyone of the three steps it took me to get from my living room to my kitchen and found a pot of coffee steaming on the countertop. I pulled my favorite mug out the cupboard and poured myself a third fix. I sat down beside June and looked at her expectedly.

"How was your day?" June asked.

My second loaded question of the day. June never asked me how my day was unless she was holding something back and needed me to cushion the blow by going on at the mouth first.

"Why don't you just tell me what's on your mind, wifey?"

Wifey? Yeah, I know. I'd been watching too much BET. June let the moniker go, though, which should have tipped me off. But I what can I say? I was dense — thickened by love. That's my story, and I'm sticking to it.

"Well, today was shaping up to be another uneventful day until I realized after you left this morning I hadn't had my period in awhile."

Fuck.

"So, that's a good thing right? I mean, it's not exactly something you or I look forward to, right?"

Lame, I know.

"You could say that, but it also alerts me that everything is as it should be — that no unexpected circumstances might arouse."

Arouse. She said arouse. I'm a 12-year-old, I know.

"What unexpected circumstances?"

Hey, I'm just following the script.

"I haven't felt good for the last few days."

"Yeah, but I thought that was from the Chinese food the other night."

"I thought so too, but I wanted be sure. So I took a home pregnancy test."

"And?"

"Well, first your mother and I have decided we're going to have a family picnic. You know, so both families can finally meet each other."

This I could deal with.

"And second?"

"I'm pregnant."

Oh, *fuck*. Fuck *me*. Fuckity, fuck fuck *fuck*.

"That's great," I said. I wrapped her in my arms because I didn't know what else to do.

God is a spiteful bitch.

Book Three:
Enoch Was A Kiss-ass

ONE

I didn't sleep well. It was all I could do to keep my mouth shut about the baby around June. It's not that I didn't *want* the baby so much as we didn't *plan* for it. I was going to go out of my mind if I didn't talk to somebody about it soon. So I did what in retrospect was probably the stupidest thing I could have done — I called my brother Ron for advice. But I will say this for my brother: He dropped what he was doing and said he would meet me in Norman the next day. I should have been wary of my brother's sudden want to come to my aid, but I was too flustered and scatter-brained to think about it. I was so flustered, in fact, that I never gave a second thought to the place he wanted to meet. It was only after I walked into the joint that I realized I was in one of the last places I wanted to be to have this conversation. But on way to my Bro-Up, I ran into one of those people God puts on Earth to test the limits of our self-control. Why? I needed to have my fix. One day, God or man

— yeah, this would definitely be a manmade invention — will create a way for us all to casually take caffeine straight into the vein, but until then I will have to visit Brown Stain and the dreaded long-haired freak.

I waited in line for about ten minutes — a long wait by Norman coffee shop standards — to be accosted by Steve the barista once again. "Como esta, dream quitter? That's Spanish for The fuck do you want?"

"I'd like a tall caffé mocha."

"No. Pick something else."

Oh, no. Not this shit again.

"Really, are we back to that?"

"Look, dream quitter, it has fallen to me to see to it that you know there are more things in life than the Bold Pick of the Day, whatever god-awful concoction you innovated that one day, and your now traditional caffé mocha. So pick something else."

"Fine. How 'bout an espresso macchiato and one of those chocolate chip cookies?"

"Wow, an espresso and a cookie all without a fight? You must be stressed out. Yeah, I can see that shit in your eyes. You look like you haven't slept in days, dream quitter."

Someone behind me tapped me on the shoulder. It was a kid dressed in a red flannel shirt, blue jeans and derelict sneakers who looked like he was in a hurry. "Are you going to be long? I have to go to class, you know?"

"I'm sorry," I said as apologetically as I could. "I'm done here."

"No you're not," Steve said. "You have to stay here and tell me what's wrong with you. Is it the job? What about the wife? She probably wants kids right about now, doesn't she?"

I swallowed hard. I didn't want to have that conversation, and I especially didn't want to have it with a guy who could probably do a damn decent cover of Smells Like Teen Spirit. "Okay, Steve. I know you're the boss of me, and I know you hold the keys to the magically flavored crack you sell behind the counter, but I really don't want to talk about this with you right now. I really just want my espresso and my cookie and to get the fuck out of here." I said every word, uttered every syllable, with a smile on my face and in a congenial tone.

I watched Steve's eyes grow to the size of jawbreakers and his expression changed to something akin to portraying — dare I say it — sympathy.

The kid behind me tapped me on the shoulder, this time with more force and at a much higher level on the Pissed-Off-O-Meter. "Buddy, the rest of us," he said, pointing to the growing herd of tweens behind him, "have places to go and things to do. So if you could just move your ass—"

"Hey!" Steve bellowed. "I'm trying to have a heart-to-heart with one of our most loyal and valued customers. Be quiet you All-American Reject wannabe, or I will not serve you anymore caffeinated heroine. Ever."

"You can't do that," the kid said.

"Oh, yeah? No more coffee for you. There. Did it. Now get the hell out of my shop before I call Hot Topic and have them repo those fucked off clothes you're wearing, you fucking poseur." The kid put his head down, turned around and walked out of the coffee shop. "Anybody else want to interrupt my conversation with a valued customer?" It sounded more like a threat than a question. "I thought so," he said after hearing nothing but the low whine of the espresso machine. "Now," Steve said, facing me. "Why don't you want to talk about it?"

Okay, after all that, I couldn't just be an ass to him.

"Well to be honest with you, Steve, I'm supposed to have the conversation you want me to have with you with my big brother not ten minutes from right now. It would only be fair that I give him a shot first, seeing as he is my brother and all."

Steve shook his head, as if everything I had said had just magically made all the sense in the world to him. "No, no. I can respect that shit, dream quitter. I never had a big brother. I had a ferret once. His name was Federico, Federico Ferret. But I just called him Fed for short, you know, like a nickname. I used to tell Fed everything. He was my best friend. He was the only one I could say shit to. He understood me. I get that shit for real, dream quitter." He wiped away a few tears, and a little snot, then a lot of snot. "You know, if you brother doesn't work out, I'm here for you, dream quitter. I'll take you out back, and we can hit the peace pipe while we talk about life, and the failures that abound in it."

"Thanks, Steve." I think that was the correct reply.

"No problem, dream quitter. I'll have one of my slaves make your espresso and heat up your cookie. Those motherfuckers are nasty coming straight out of the freezer."

My espresso and cookie came quickly. I drained the espresso right there at the pick-up stand and wolfed down the cookie. I left the shop and headed down Asp when God sent yet another human being to test me because, clearly, Steve had not performed the task appointed to him.

"Mikey McNulty, just the man I'm here to see," he said, throwing his arms up, overstating the moment.

It was fucking Jake Mishkin. He was dressed in a gray suit I assumed was tailored by some pencil-necked dick named Tally Tailor McTails in New York who probably spoke with an Italian accent and walked around with a tape measure draped around his neck like an ornamental scarf. His shoes were shined, and what used to be his Jewfro was lathered up with enough hair moose to burn down the whole of Asp Avenue. He reached out his hand. I resisted the urge to spit in it and merely shook it. What a shame because I could have probably worked up something chewy and yellow for him.

"What are you doing here," I said. "Aren't you supposed to be in New York?"

"I am actually. But your mom called my mom, and so forth and so on, and now I'm here for the picnic on Saturday. By the way, congratulations. You picked a good one."

I wanted to rip his spine from his body and show it to him as he died on the sidewalk beneath my shoe. "Thanks, Jake. We're both very happy."

"I hope so. Frankly, I was surprised to hear your mother is taking it so well."

"Taking what well?"

"You know, you being married to one of the blacks. But I guess the day you told her you were married is the day June became a dark-skinned white girl."

Oh no that asshole didn't?!

"She's a very understanding woman, my mother," I said. "She knows two people in love when she sees them."

"I'm happy to hear it, 'ol boy. But between you and me, you're not supposed to marry that girl. It's okay to date her, hell, even sleep with her, but you don't marry her. I never really thought you'd follow through with your jungle fever but damn. I heard you brought her to church too. My mother would have skinned me alive if I brought a black to Synagogue."

This is the part where I count backward from ten, right?

"My wife is a wonderful woman. My mother is wonderful woman. I am blessed to have two women in my life who are as understanding as they are."

Blessed? Who the fuck am I? Billy Graham?

"I think that's just your Catholic guilt talking, Mikey."

No, it's not. I hope.

"Anyway," Jake said, "I'm on my way to see my parents. I've decided to make a holiday of it and leave all my work in New York behind. It'll be fun to pick up where I left off and poke around with old friends again."

He said poke, right? What do you think he meant when he said poke?

"I'm sure everyone will enjoy catching up with you," I said. "I sure have."

I'll confess it later out of habit, but as things stand, I think God will let that one slide. We're even. I mean, He created Jake Mishkin.

Jake started to walk away, but stopped and turned back. "Remember to tell your lovely wife hello for me."

I gritted my teeth, clinched my fists and managed to say, "Sure thing." Jake smiled back at me and swaggered away. I waited there on the sidewalk, staring down the street until I thought I had reached a reasonable level of tranquility. God knows if I had met up with my brother in the state Jake had immediately left me in, I would have said or done something stupid. My brother is not the person to do stupid things in front of. I swear the man can't remember who the sixteenth president is, but he can recall the night I woke up with something gooey and moist in my shorts. I had to have Pappy explain to me what a wet dream was and how I should "take care of manly tendencies." (My Pappy's remedy involved a bottle of warm lotion, a box of tissues and a black and white photo of Rita Hayworth as Gilda.) Yes, I was quite glad to have calmed down before I met up with Ron. He was Captain Obvious after all.

"What you really mean when you say she's pregnant is—"

"I don't know any other way to say it, Ron. She said she's pregnant. I can't be anymore literal than that."

"The bun is in the oven; play time is over; her perky puppies are about to become sagging dogs; the snatch widens?"

I guess I was wrong. It turns out I could have been more literal after all.

"Yeah, that's what she said. And I don't know what to do. By the way, I don't feel entirely comfortable having this conversation here."

"What are you talking about?" Ron said, gesturing to the surroundings. "This is a fine establishment, one of the finest establishments in this wretched college town if ever there was one."

My brother also moonlights as Captain Delusional.

"Chesty's is a strip joint, plain and simple," I said. "There is no fine quality to it, unless your definition of fine includes rhinestone g-strings, breast large enough that they could be confused with inflatables in the Macy's parade, and music that makes you feel as if you're permanently stuck in the 90s."

Ron made a face at me as if to ask what other definition of fine I could be referring to. He turned back to the dancer who was presently entertaining him, looking like a mesmerized 3-year-old who had seen something sparkly for the first time. My big brother had been bringing me to Chesty's since he and I were old enough to be confused for of-age college kids. I never liked being in there for a variety of reasons. The first one was for religious reasons. I mean, lust is a sin; always has been, always will be. How can any straight-man walk into a strip club full of women in thongs and bikinis who were working their way through school — every stripper at Chesty's had the same story, even 38-year-old Janice, "The Hussy with too much Hubris" — and not feel like he broke the tenth all-inclusive commandment. You know the one I mean: Thou shall not covet thy neighbor's [insert object here]. These girls were someone's daughters, and in some cases I'm sure, someone's wife. It was still relatively early in the evening to be in a strip joint in Vegas, let alone Norman, so the club was rather empty save my brother, a few dancers, the midget bouncer, bartender and one other poor old schmuck who felt just fine about eating at a strip club. Me? I'm not eating off the same surface that someone's raw ass has slid across on multiple occasions. Herpes is for life.

I tapped my brother on the shoulder, trying to pry his attention back from the bountiful set of boobs bouncing in his face. He shoved a single in between the stripper's breasts, smiled and turned to me.

"You're married, you know," I said.

Ron furrowed his brow, as if I had said something patently untrue. "Why do you have to be such a party-pooper? Besides, Mary-Katherine knows."

"Your wife knows you're at a strip joint shoving dollar bills down some co-ed's cleavage?"

"No. She knows I'm here taking my little brother out for the bachelor party he never had."

"I never wanted a bachelor party."

"You see? That's your problem. You're too selfish."

"I'm selfish?"

"Yes, you're selfish. A bachelor party isn't for the groom."

"It isn't?"

"No. A bachelor party is for the groom's friends and his groomsmen."

"You're sure about that?"

"Absolutely. A bachelor party is for married men to remember the good 'ol days — the days when we wolves used to prowl the woods freely. Now, the only time we get to go out on the hunt is when the wife tells us we're out of milk."

"You're making too much out of this. Besides, if this were a real bachelor party, wouldn't my friends be here?"

"I can make some calls if it makes you feel better."

"No, I don't want to see anybody else. For that matter, I never asked you to come up here in the first place."

"I just wanted to help my brother in need."

"You wanted to get away from Mary-Katherine for a few days."

"That too. The woman has become our mother. Who wants to marry their mother?"

I shook my head knowingly. "You will never change, Ron."

"She'll be up here in a few days anyway. She's even going to bring the rugrats. Enough about me and why I decided to help you deal with this matter personally. Do you know if you're going to be a daddy or not?"

"I told you already. June is pregnant."

"Things aren't like they were when we were kids. Women have a mind of their own now. They're bodies are their property, or so they tell us. She might not want to be a mommy, if you catch my drift."

I hadn't thought of that. No, really. The thought hadn't even crossed my mind. I always just thought we would have the baby. I mean, I just got a raise. We were both employed. My apartment — *our* apartment — was shit, but we would be able to move into a nicer place soon if we saved and cut back on, I don't know, tap water. We could make it work.

"Nah, she wouldn't do that," I said. "I doubt she's even thinking of doing such a thing."

"Maybe, but are you sure?" Ron said, lifting his glass of Jameson's to stress his point. "Can you really say beyond a shadow of a doubt that you know what your wife is thinking? Can you really say you know what goes on in the horribly complex wonderment that is a woman's mind?"

I didn't have to say anything.

Ron smiled at me and said, "Welcome to the life of a married man."

"So how do I find out?"

"Have you thought about asking her if she's going to keep it?"

"I can't do that. No man can do that. I mean, I could, but who would want to. Then again, I've read articles about women who get offended if their men don't ask and others that get just as offended if they do."

"Another conundrum associated with the ever-evolving jigsaw puzzle that is the woman's brain. Damned if you do, damned if you don't."

"If it were Mary-Katherine, what would you do?"

Ron stared at me hard for a few seconds. I could see him mulling over whether or not he would tell me seriously. He emptied his drink and dropped it on the dancer's stage.

"I asked her once," he said. "It was about our oldest. I spent the next six months going to marriage counseling, followed by my being served divorced papers. She made me move out. I stayed at a Motel 6 for two weeks before she let me move back into my own house. She even called mom. But hey, at least I know not to ask again, and my marriage is still intact. But June, June is different. She may be completely okay with you asking."

What followed his sentiments was the longest, most deeply satisfying and unnerving two minutes of silence I had ever shared with my brother. He had turned out to be not-so-flawless and brilliant, and yet, it was his finest big brother moment of our sibling rivalry. I will always love him for that.

"Either way, someone is going to have to tell mom about it," Ron said. "You know how she wanted us all to be like Enoch. God knows what dad will say."

"First off, Enoch was a kiss-ass. And second, why the hell would I do something stupid like that? No, I reached my quota for stupid decisions after I called you."

"Suit yourself. But if mom or dad find out during the picnic, it's your ass, not mine."

"Until then, you're going to keep your mouth shut."

"Is that a threat, little brother?"

"Let me put it this way: If you tell mom or dad June's pregnant, Mary-Katherine will find out you're Chesty's best out-of-state patron."

Did I just stoop that low to keep my mother and father from finding out my wife is pregnant? You're damn right I did.

"But that just keeps my mouth closed. What are you going to do about June?"

"You let me handle my wife," I said. Though I hadn't the slightest clue how I was going to handle her. It's not as if I could make her an offer she couldn't refuse. "Now, do you want another drink?"

"No, but you do — and a dance. I'll be damned if my little brother doesn't get a lap dance at his bachelor party." Ron rose to his feet and started marching around Chesty's looking for a worthy stripper.

"I don't want one," I said. "I'm married now. The bachelor party is supposed to come before the wedding, not months later."

"Shut up, little brother. I'm looking for a good one." Ron passed by three women working the pole before he stopped in front of a blonde who had just come on stage. Under the stage lights she looked gorgeous; powder green eyes, long flowing hair and a figure reminiscent of Ms. Monroe.

"Say Chesty. Get it? Chesty?" My brother laughed at his own joke. It's times like these when I would rather not claim him. "How do you feel about giving my brother a dance?"

Remember what I said about how much I love my brother? I take it all back.

She looked me up and down, then looked back at Ron. "Well?" he said. "He ain't gonna bite. He lost his virginity just a few months ago. He's harmless."

At that moment, I wanted to stab him with business end of a machete — in the eye.

"Ron, really, you don't have to do this," I said.

"The cost is twenty bucks for ten minutes," she said to Ron.

"Whew," Ron said, "Twenty bucks for ten minutes. That's good work if you can get it."

"Ron—"

"Shut up, little brother. Darling, here's forty, and please, be gentle with him."

She snatched the wad of cash from Ron and came down off the stage. I looked at Ron incredulously.

"What?" he said. "I just want you to have a good time."

"What am I going to tell June?"

"Are you stupid or something? You never tell your wife about getting a lap dance."

"No, I meant about being pregnant."

"Oh, that's on you. I can't help you there."

"Gee, thanks."

"Anytime."

The dancer came from the back and took my hand. "Are we gonna do this or what?" she said.

Ron smiled and twiddled his fingers. "Have a good time you two."

TWO

I followed the dancer into a private room adjacent to the bar. She sat me down in a single chair in the middle of what amounted to a broom closet and latched the door. She turned around, leaned against the door and draped her hand over her head like a centerfold in an issue of *Playboy* — not that I know what a centerfold in *Playboy* looks like, I just . . . Fuck it. She was hot and sexy and I found myself having to cross my legs and do my damndest to think of anything else.

"How do you want me?" she said. She slinked closer to me, putting her hands on the arms of the chair and licked her lips. Believe it or not, this was my umpteenth time in a strip club and I had never once got a lap dance, so to be completely honest, this was to be my first. Wait, that was a pivotal moment, wasn't it? It was the moment I realized I had failed as a 23-year-old male to do what most 20-something men accomplished by their late teens. But that couldn't be *all* my fault, could it? I mean, there was no Catholic preparatory school in Norman. If there was, I would have surely been made to attend it along with my brother and sister. If I had gone to a Catholic prep school I would have had an increased chance of meeting, kissing and eventually fondling a naughty Catholic school girl who would have probably given me a lap dance by tenth grade. Yes, my logic is sound enough to make me feel like less of a failure in the lap dance department.

"This is my first time," I said. "This is my first time in here, well, not in Chesty's, but in one of these rooms. I've just been, uh, been busy for the past twenty-three years or so."

Did I just say I've been too busy to get a lap dance? I am fucking retarded.

She smiled and came within inches of my nose. "Why don't you just sit back, relax and let me do the heavy-lifting? Just remember to keep your hands to yourself, okay?"

I chose to nod my head yes this time, lest I do something more to prove my inexperience. She turned around slowly and sat down right on top of my crotch. Yes, that action would help matters tremendously now, wouldn't it?

She leaned back against me. Her head fell back on my shoulder. Then I felt a slow burn begin in my crotch that was quickly becoming a flame. I stood her up because if I hadn't, this story would have ended much worse than it began.

"What's wrong?" she said.

"Nothing. I just . . . I don't know you're name."

Hey, on short notice, that was pretty good.

"My name?" she said.

"Yes, I think I would feel better about this if I knew your name."

I could see her thinking about it and then she said, "I guess that's okay. My name is Constance."

"Constance? Constance what?"

"Constance Jo Bennett."

"Constance," I said again, rolling the name around in my head.

She folded her arms and backed away. "Yeah, Constance. As in daughter of William the Conqueror. You have a problem with my name?"

"I meant no disrespect."

"Then what *did* you mean?"

"I was just taken aback by your name. That's all. I know it well."

"How's that?"

"You're also the namesake of the daughter of Constantine the Great, the Roman Emperor. She was a saint, you see, and two of her virtues were ideals that I was taught to honor: fortitude and faith. But she was spotted and ugly, and you don't have spots."

She scrunched up her face.

"But you're not ugly either. You're actually extremely pretty; Helen of Troy pretty; stained glass window pretty." I really have to work on keeping my foot out of my mouth.

"Are you religious or something?"

"Guilty," I said, raising my hand. "I was raised Roman Catholic."

"Raised. You aren't anymore?"

"Actually, I'm a bit too Catholic for my own good sometimes."

Understatement of the year nominee, that sentence, but on the bright side Constance no longer looked like she wanted to take off her six-inch glass stiletto and stab me in the neck with it.

"What's your name?"

"Me? I'm Mikey."

She extended her hand, and I shook it. "It's nice to meet you, Mikey. Now, do you want to get back to business, or what?"

I looked around the dark broom closet, then at the single lamplight swinging overhead and then back to Constance. "Is it all right if we just talk?"

"Talk?"

"Yeah, you can keep the money—"

"I know I can the money."

"Yeah," I said, grabbing the back of my neck. "And you can tell my brother whatever you think you should tell him after we leave this place."

"Is he going to be out there waiting on us, or something?" Constance said.

"Knowing him, absolutely. He'll be expecting a full report."

"Your brother sounds like a real asshole."

"Sometimes. But he's a good enough guy."

She leaned back up against the wall. "I heard you're having a kid."

"Where'd you hear that?" I sounded more defensive than I had intended.

"Out by the stage. You two seemed be arguing about it. Should I say congratulations?"

"Oh, yeah, sure," I said. "Having a baby is supposed to be a happy event."

"Yeah, it's supposed to be. But is it?"

"Yes. It is.

"Then congratulations, Mikey."

"Thank you. I'm happy about it."

"Is your wife?"

"Who said I was married?"

"You told me you're a good Catholic boy. I just assumed you were."

"Your assumption is correct. And she's just fine about it."

"Fine? That doesn't sound like any happy pregnant woman I ever met?"

"You haven't met my wife."

"Don't get defensive. You're the one who said you wanted to talk."

"But I don't want to talk about me. Are you married?"

"Nope. I don't see the point."

"The point of what? The point of getting married?"

"Have you ever loved anyone?"

"Sure. I love my parents."

"I mean, have you ever loved another man . . . or woman if you're so inclined."

"I like men, and no, I have never loved a man. I view them like ranchers view cows — they're pieces of meat to be enjoyed. No offense."

"None taken. Are you in school?"

"What, because I work at a strip club and it's close to campus, I must be working here to put myself through school?"

"I just thought—"

"You thought wrong, Mikey. Leave it."

"It's left. How much more time do we have to stay in here until it will appear you've done your duty?"

"I'd say we're good in about two minutes."

"Are you always this much fun to talk to?"

"If you weren't married, I'd tell you to buy me a drink after my shift ends and you could find out just how much fun I really am. But you are."

She said the last sentence with such an air of finality that all I could think to say was, "Okay." If I had said anything else, at the time, I think it would have bordered on infidelity. How very Catholic of me. Constance unlatched the door and walked out first. I followed closely behind — but not too closely. Ron was sitting right outside the door waiting on us, his drink in his lap, mesmerized by none other than The Hussy with too much Hubris.

"It's amazing to see a woman that age that can still move like that," he said. "How'd it go?"

Constance turned to me, then to Ron. "Your brother was amazing," she said, and walked off toward the dressing room.

Ron turned to me. I had only once seen him so flabbergasted, and that was the day he learned he contracted his first case of syphilis. "You didn't," he said.

I shrugged my shoulders. "A gentleman never tells," even when there is nothing to tell. At all.

After jabbering back and forth for a few minutes about my brother's need to know details, we started toward the door. I went to open it, but the door sprang open, and my dad came striding through it. He caught sight of us just as quickly as we had of him, and the most awkward thirty seconds of silence two sons and a father can share took place.

"Ron," my father said.

"Dad," Ron said.

"What are you doing here, dad?" I said.

My father said nothing. In fact, he wasn't even looking at me. He looked around, and finally came back to my face. "I was just leaving," he said clearly to my brother and not to me. He opened the door again and walked out. I was about to follow him when my brother grabbed me by the arm.

"Let him go, Mikey."

I turned toward my brother. "Why won't he talk to me? What don't I know?"

"Nothing. He and mom probably just had another fight is all. You know how he gets after he's had a few. Just let it go."

I studied him for a few moments, and I could see he was holding something back, but I didn't think Chesty's was the place to talk about it just then, which is ironic if you consider what we were there to talk about in the first place. "Fine," I said. "But you're going to tell me what you know before the picnic."

THREE

At work the next day, I did my best to avoid Marty. I wanted to avoid him because, well, Marty is just one more pimple on the ass of life, and I was late on a story that should have been filed while I was having a heart-to-heart with my brother. I had just made it to my desk, picked up my tape recorder, reporter's notebook and pen and turned around to leave when Marty appeared inches from my face.

"Where the fuck is my feature on that barber, McNulty?" The air-conditioner had been shut off to save money — in July — so Marty was sweating more than usual. "I wanted that story filed last night. Why the hell isn't it in front of a copy editor?"

"I'm on my way there now. I just needed to pick up some things."

He folded his arms and a bead of sweat dropped from his stubbly chin onto his rolled up shirt sleeve. His pits were stained and I was quite sure he wasn't wearing an under shirt under his white button-down.

"You're on your way now. You're on your way *right now* to report a story I told you to have written by four o'clock *yesterday*. This is why I wanted to pick my own guy. Your piece is supposed go below the fold in tomorrow's edition. But now the entire team of copy editors and designers will have to wait on you because you were probably getting smashed at some Mick dive. I swear, if that piece isn't filed by four o'clock today, the chief and I are going to go looking for a new features reporter. Now get out of my face."

I could have argued with him on several points, especially the one about me being at some Mick dive. Chesty's is a lot of things, but it ain't exactly where an Irishman would go to drown his sorrows — the neon lights alone would drive him bat-shit crazy. So instead of arguing with him, I simply smiled and left the newsroom as quickly as I could, keeping my head down the whole way.

As soon as I came to my piece-of-shit-on-wheels, I cranked up the air-conditioning. There were a lot of things wrong with that car, but thankfully the air-conditioning wasn't one of them. I let the cool air blow over my face for a few minutes, and then put the car in gear.

The barbershop I was headed to was located on the south side of Norman off 24th Avenue and Lindsey, next to Interstate-35. I had been there many times before, but this would be my first time going there to write a story, though I had always wanted to. The barbers knew me — mostly because I'm pretty sure I'm the only white boy who frequented the shop — and that would make things a little bit easier. However, if LaRon wasn't around I would have to keep my "motherfucking mouth shut, or get blasted on" as LaRon's other barber, Faruk, like to frequently say to me when LaRon was out of the shop. Whether or not Faruk had a gun on him, I never really knew. But each time I walked into the shop I made sure LaRon was around before I opened my mouth.

It didn't take too long for me to make the drive from downtown Norman to The Hook-up Style Shop. After all, Norman isn't that big a city. Seriously, the square radius of Norman has to be smaller than most outlet malls. I pulled into the blue and white office buildings the shop was located in and parked. I checked my passenger seat to make sure I had everything I needed — reporter's notebook, pen and tape recorder. I never felt safe walking into an interview with just one set of note-taking tools. I wouldn't ever know until I was about to ask my first question whether or not I felt more comfortable writing in shorthand or putting my recorder in between the interviewee and me. I stepped out of the car and put the pen behind my ear, the notebook in my back pocket, opposite of my wallet and the recorder in my right pants pocket. I touched each space to make sure everything was as it should be. Don't judge me. It's my system. I'm sure you've got your system, too.

I opened the door and walked in to the sound of "Welcome to The Hook-up Style Shop, please write your name down on the notepad and we'll be with you in a mom— Oh, it's just the white boy," Faruk said, looking up from the head he was cutting. "You slumming with us colored folk again?"

Faruk had on his usually attire: black combat boots, military fatigues, a black shirt twice his size with a large marijuana leaf screened on it and a gold chain ornamented with a gold fist on end around his neck. The lay person might describe Faruk as militant. Faruk described himself in, uh, different terms. There were three men waiting on haircuts, one in Faruk's chair and no sign of LaRon.

"I'm here on a story this time. Is LaRon around?"

"Don't talk to me like you know me, white devil."

It doesn't matter that Faruk and I probably listen to the same music. It doesn't matter that we probably agree on most political issues. Under different circumstances I probably would have complimented Faruk on his fist chain. But none of that mattered. What mattered to Faruk? I was a white male and married to "one of our Nubian queens." This was the part where I shut the fuck up and let Faruk do his thing, or "I be fucked."

"Three hundred years you and yours have oppressed my people," Faruk said. "Since before the Mayflower, you have done your best to enslave the black man. And in the process we lost our share of martyrs; Gabrielle Processor, Huey P., James Cheney, Dr. Martin Luther the King to say nothing of the women you raped and killed along the way. And for what? So that we could have rights your founding fathers claimed were inalienable. You know what? I ought to take the clippers to your neck. We wouldn't be even with the white devil, but at least I'd feel better."

"Look, man. I just need to speak with LaRon. That's all."

"Well, LaRon ain't here," Faruk said, gesturing to the room. "You're stuck with me and the bruhs, snow flake."

Okay, seriously, what would you do here? I was in a hostile environment with a hostile human being who outweighs me by a good one hundred and fifty pounds. The patrons waiting on haircuts were all giving me the evil eye. I stood frozen in the center of the room, watching these men shoot lasers through my forehead. I was cooking in my own flop sweat, praying Faruk didn't pull out the AR-15 — equipped with a shell-catcher and night vision — I just knew was hidden behind his barber's chair. I closed my eyes and readied myself to choke on my own blood.

"Faruk, will you shut that shit up. You know Mikey is good people."

LaRon had just come through the door — thank God — with a bag of goodies from Natural Grocers in hand and sat them down in his chair. I gave him a look of thanks, and he waved it off.

"I'm on that healthy-living kick," he said. "I got to get some of this weight off me some way." LaRon was a big man, pushing three pounds at about six-foot-five. It was strange to see a man of his size anywhere holding a bag of anything, but handling a bag from Natural Grocers took it to whole other level. He had on a big red polo, jean shorts and a pair of Jordan's. Ordinarily I would make a crack about him resembling the Kool-aid man, but in light of the company that surrounded me, I thought better of it.

"How you doing, Mikey?" LaRon said. He began rifling through the bag and pulled out a large apple, sat the bag on the ground and dug in. When LaRon chews, the shop crunches.

"I'm good," I said. I still felt a little shaky watching Faruk out of the corner of my eye.

"I heard our boy is looking pretty good for the draft in a year," LaRon said.

He was referring to Anthony. Anthony was not only the pride of Stark High; he was the pride of every man in the Norman area who called himself a basketball fan.

"He did," I said. "He put up 32 in a developmental tournament a few weeks ago."

"You think he's got something?"

"If he keeps playing the way they did against Booker T., I don't know that there is a man in the pro's that can play with him."

That brought smile to his face, which is good. It's always better to interview someone when they're in a good mood — they are more likely to say something they normally wouldn't. I'm no different from any other reporter. I love a good quote as much as the next guy.

"So, it doesn't look like you came in here to get a haircut. I mean, I cut you up just a week ago, which reminds me, I never asked how you and June are doing."

Faruk turned his nose up at the mention of June.

"We're good, life is good." A white lie I will confess soon, promise.

"That's good. Marriage is God's gift to us all. I'm glad you and June are enjoying that gift."

"That mixing of melanin is an unholy union!" Faruk said. "It ain't right. The minister says—"

"Will shut up, you up tight no pussy-getting negro," LaRon said. "Who this man chooses to marry and who chooses to marry *him* is of no concern to you bean-pie-eating motherfuckers. Now cut that man's head. *Da*mn."

I rubbed the back of my neck, trying not to look guilty. "Anyway, do you know why I'm here?"

"It wouldn't have anything to do with that damn championship, would it?"

"It would."

"They really want you to write about that for the paper?"

"They do."

"But I thought you wrote about sports? You're the reason I pick up the paper most days — you and Anthony's box score."

"I appreciate that, but I was promoted. I'm the features news reporter at the Sentinel now. And my assignment is to write about you and your winning that championship."

"What if I don't want to talk about it?"

"Then you would make me look real bad at my job."

"I don't want to do that. I understand a man having a job to do. All right, what you got?" he said, plopping down in his barber's chair.

I pulled out my tape recorder and placed it on the arm of his chair. "How long have you been bowling?"

"Since my daddy first gave me a ball and a pair of shoes and set me out on the lane at about six years old."

"Had you ever bowled in a professional tournament before?"

"No, never. I always bowled because I liked it, and it made my daddy happy to watch me do it."

"Your dad is a big influence on your life?"

"Was," LaRon said. "He *was* a big influence on my life, but he ain't with us no more."

"Was he a barber too?"

"Nah, he was an accountant. Once he figured out I liked bowling, he thought he'd keep me in it. I guess he figured if I could keep score at a bowling alley, I could become a pretty good CPA too. But we both know that ain't how it works."

"He didn't bowl?"

"Hell no. My daddy hated the inside of a bowling alley. He only liked it because I was good at it."

"Have you ever thought about turning pro?"

"Nope, never. I got my barber's license when I turned eighteen. I bought this shop with the money I saved when I turned twenty-nine, and God has granted me a good living with good customers. Why would I want to change that?"

"So why did you decide to compete in the PBA Tulsa Classic?"

"That's simple. I lost a bet to Brother Minister Kill Whitey over here," LaRon said, pointing toward Faruk.

"Better to be called Kill Whitey than by my slave name," Faruk said. "The white devil will rue the day he stepped foot onto the motherland."

"As always, you're gonna have to forgive Faruk, and let that shit slide. I think his mother sipped Old English when she was pregnant with him. Anyway, I lost a bet to Faruk there, who has seen me bowl before and knows I hate competing. He made me a bet that he could lose more weight than me in a week. If he did, I would have to compete in that stupid tournament and listen to him rant about the nation of Islam and attend his services for a week. If I won, he would have to wear a pink Britney Spears shirt, white khakis and boat shoes for a week."

"And you see who Allah allowed to be the victor," Faruk broke in. "The minister says—"

"Will you shut up about Allie Ackbar? No one wants to hear the minister's thoughts on the subject. I listened to you talk that bowtie gospel shit. I even went to temple with you. Now shut the *hell* up."

"You ain't gonna punk me like this in front of Wonder Bread over there when I get my own shop."

"Well you ain't got your own shop. You still work in *my* shop, and as long as you do, you're gonna keep that shit to yourself in my presence."

Faruk left well enough alone and went back to the head he was cutting.

"You got anymore questions for me, Mikey?" LaRon said.

"How did it feel to bowl against Webber in the finals?"

"Like I was bowling with Gerald Mays down a Sooner Lanes — they both talk a lot of shit."

"Thanks, LaRon," I said. "It should be in tomorrow's paper."

LaRon nodded his head, and I turned to Faruk. "Can you speak to the character of LaRon as a boss and friend?"

"He's one cold-ass nigga, a honky-hater. A down brother of the highest order in this reality dominated by old, corporate white men and their never-ending need to pillage their fellow man and rape Mother Nature's delicious bosom. Now, print that shit."

I asked for that.

I clicked off the tape recorder and said goodbye to LaRon, then walked out of the shop to my car. I opened the door. Well, I tried to open the door. It was locked. My keys and phone were staring up at me from the driver's seat. Yes, I am now the idiot who checks himself before going into a place — Twice! — and still manages to lock himself out of his car. These are the things I prayed God wouldn't let happen to me, especially on deadline. I could grovel, but Enoch was a kiss-ass. After cursing myself out for about two minutes I sauntered back into the shop and asked LaRon if I could use his phone. He gave me the cordless without hesitation and I called Triple A. It's by pure luck that I still have a membership. The operator informed me it was due to expire the next day, and then he told me they would send a locksmith close to the area to help me out. Rather than stay inside the shop with Faruk — even under the protection of LaRon — I decided to bake in one hundred degree heat while I waited the half-hour it took for a wrecker to appear in the parking lot. What happened next was unexpected, to put it mildly.

FOUR

Constance stepped out of the white wrecker with Earl Pearl's Automotive Repair and Tow painted on it in red, white and blue cursive. She was dressed in black steel toes, torn blue jeans and a white tank top, covered by a blue jean shirt. Her hair was pulled back into a ponytail and her cheeks were stained with oil smudges. She walked up to me, this time void of glamorous sexiness, and only your run-of-the-mill sexiness. (Yes, there is a difference.)

"Hey, you're the guy who had never had a lap dance before I gave you one?" Constance said.

Guilty as charged.

I answered her with a dumbfounded look.

"What? You think humping a pole at Chesty's pays the bills? Not in this city, not in this state. I'd have to move to Texas before I could make any real money."

She had a point. I mean, Oklahoma is the buckle on the Bible belt.

"I just didn't expect to see you."

"What's your name again?"

"You don't remember my name. Just that I hadn't had a lap dance."

"I would if you had tipped well."

Fair enough.

"I'm Mikey."

"Oh, yeah, Mikey, that's it. Do you know of anyone here who called for a locksmith?" Constance said.

I raised my hand.

"You?" she said.

"Yeah, me."

"Where's your car?"

I pointed to the piece of shit behind me. "I managed to lock my keys and my phone in there," I said. "Triple-A said they were sending someone."

She looked it over. "You have a 1999 Oldsmobile Alero, two-door, automatic — a real piece of shit."

See? Told you.

"Yes, I've known that from the very beginning. Anyway, do you think you can help me out?"

"I'll be right back," Constance said. She walked to her truck, opened the door and pulled out a thin piece of metal from under the driver's side seat. She came back to the car and shoved the metal down the side of my car's driver's side window. "I'm fishing for the catch," she said. It didn't take her long to find it. In less than thirty seconds, she had the door popped and open.

"Thanks," I said.

"No problem, it's nice to be able to leave the crowbar in the car and help someone out in this profession every once in awhile."

"Crowbar?"

"Sometimes I run into people who just won't let a repo woman do her job."

"Repo woman. Like you go out and repossess other people's cars?"

"They aren't their's if they don't make the payments. Besides, repo is half of Earl's business." She sounded a tad defensive when she said that, so I chose not to pursue it further.

"Well, thanks for your help again."

"Don't mention it."

I reached for my phone first. It was dead. I chalked that one up to my inability to stay in the office long enough to charge it. I put the key in the ignition and turned it over. Nothing. I tried again. Still nothing. I knew next to nothing about cars, and I figured that wasn't the time to start acting like I did. I hopped out of the car and shuffled over to the rig. I knocked on the driver's side door. I banged harder than I normally would because the engine was so loud. She rolled down the window.

"What do you need?"

"My car," I said. "It won't start."

"You do know you're supposed to put the key in the little hole and turn it, don't you?"

Everybody loves a smartass. Except Enoch. He was a kiss-ass.

"Funny. Do you think you can tow me to your garage, and do . . . whatever it is mechanics do to make cars work again?"

Yeah, those are the words that literally came fumbling out of my mouth. I was having a rough day, okay?

Constance looked at me as if I had just took a shit in her passenger seat. "It really doesn't start? You aren't doing this because you're trying to get into my pants?"

"No, no of course not — I'm married." She gave me a look like my being married accounted for less than nothing. "I'm not trying to get into your pants, and my car is seriously broken. I swear."

She smiled. "Good Catholic boys shouldn't swear."

Yeah, tell me about it.

"So, are you going to help me?"

"Yeah, I'll tow you to the garage, but if you try anything — like accidentally fall on top of me and your hand happens to land on my boob — I'm going to take my crowbar and show your balls my best Albert Pujols impression. Got it?"

I vigorously nodded my head yes and — out of pure survival instinct — checked to make sure my testicles were still where they should be and not scrambled on the pavement.

Constance hooked her rig up to my car and in a few minutes we were on the road. I sat in the passenger's side — much closer to the door than is usually my custom — and watched the road.

"Are you okay?" Constance said.

"I'm fine."

"You don't look fine."

"How do I look?"

"You look like you're about to start dry humping that door at any moment."

"I'm just trying to keep my end of the bargain."

"I didn't know threatening to hit men in the balls was such a good sexual harassment deterrent."

"With most men, it might not be. But me, I'm rather fond of my testicles, and I like to think they are fond of me. We look out for each other."

"Are you a little off or something?"

"Or something for sure, but lately, I think I have been a little off, yes, so probably a bit of both at the moment. Exactly where is Earl Pearl's Automotive and Tow?"

"Off Main and Porter."

"How long do you think it will take to fix my car?"

"I don't know. It'll have to be diagnosed first, and then I'm sure Earl will give you a time-frame along with a dollar amount. The tow alone is going to cost you upward of one hundred and fifty dollars and—"

"Wait. I thought Triple-A covered this?"

"Triple-A covers my car-jacking skills. The tow, the diagnosis, the parts, the labor will all come out of your pocket."

Fuck.

"You guys wouldn't happen to be able to give me a public servant discount, would you?"

"For what? You in the military?"

"I'm a reporter," I said proudly.

"Oh, you had better keep that to yourself when Earl's around. He doesn't like reporters since one of them sued him awhile back."

There goes my public servant discount.

"You wouldn't happen to have a phone charger, would you?" I said, pulling out my phone.

She took the phone out of my hand and examined it. "I don't, but Cindy might."

"Who's Cindy?"

"She's the cash register for Earl."

We pulled into the garage parking lot, and Constance let out me at the office entrance to check-in my car. I walked into the office to the sound of a jingling bell against the glass door. The room was next to empty with just two chairs and a desk in it for furniture. A gangly teenage girl in a purple Justin Bieber shirt stood behind the desk with a pink set of headphones in her hears. She was engrossed in a magazine spread across the desk. She didn't pop up when I walked in, so I eased closer to the desk. She still didn't see me. I waved my hand in between her head and the magazine. A face of anger, rage and shame ornamented with Technicolor braces accosted me.

"Can I help you?" she said through a mouth of metal and rubberbands.

"Yes, Cindy, is it?"

Her answer: the death stare.

"I'm checking in my car for a—"

"Diagnostic check," she said.

"Yes, yes, that's it," I said gleefully.

She pulled out a stack of forms and plopped them on the desk in front of me. "Fill these out," she said, putting the headphones back on.

I stopped her just before she was able to put the second earpiece in. "You wouldn't happen to have a charger I could hook this up to?" I said, producing my phone. "It's dead, and I really need to see if I have in texts or voice messages."

"No," she said followed by the death stare.

I was about to turn away and leave when I saw the charger I needed for my phone plugged into the wall behind her vacant of a phone. I waved my hand in front of her once more. I could feel her sullen, devil eyes boring a hole through my forehead.

"I hate to bother you again, but I couldn't help noticing the charger you have plugged in behind you looks exactly like the kind used to charge my phone. Do you think I could use it?"

She turned to look at the charger, as if she had never seen it there before, and then back to me. She opened her hand, and I gently placed my phone in it. I watched her hook my phone up and leave it on the ground.

I nodded my thanks and sat down in one of the chairs closest to the door. I would have asked the Justin Bieber devil child for a pen, but I didn't want to risk being the victim of some hideous wiccan magic. I used the pen I had on me to fill out the mountain of paperwork she gave me and placed it back on the desk. I tapped Cindy on the shoulder to let her know it was there, and thought better of staying in that office for another minute.

Outside, I found Constance with a lit cigarette in hand, leaning against her rig.

"It's too hot to be outside," I said.

"Maybe for someone who sits behind a desk all day. I work in the heat."

"You just don't like me very much, do you?"

"It's not that I don't like you. I don't really like anybody. People bore me."

"You prefer cats, dogs?"

"I prefer silence."

Okay, in retrospect this is the part where she probably wants me to just shut the fuck up and leave her alone. But I'm dense, a McNulty and a journalist, which means I just have to keep yapping until someone loses an eye.

"So you work at Chesty's and you work here? You really aren't in school, are you?"

"You writing a book or something?"

"No, it's just that I've run into you twice in less than twenty-four hours, and I'm making an effort to know you."

Constance threw the butt on the ground and crushed it out with the toe of her boot. "Why? I'm just the girl who grinded on your crotch and towed your car to a garage with a reputation for overcharging and taking away people's rides to work."

"If that's who you want to be to me, then I'll leave you alone."

She sighed. "All right, you first though."

"Me?"

"Yeah, you. What's your deal?"

"My deal?"

"Everybody's got one."

"My deal," I said, looking down at my shoes and stalling for time. I wasn't stalling because I didn't know what my deal was — I just didn't know how to put it tersely. This is where being a writer helps. You can revise, edit, shape and smooth the truth. Spoken word fails to illustrate the best of you.

"How much do you want to know?"

"There's that much, huh?"

"You have no idea."

"Fine, I'll be play the reporter this time and ask the questions."

This could end badly.

"How long have you been married?"

"Just over four months."

"Any kids?"

"Technically, no."

"Technically? How can you technically have kids?"

"My wife's pregnant. That's how."

"Expected?"

I hesitated. "We've been over this. Remember? At Chesty's?"

"I'm asking the questions. A love child, then?"

"No," I said quickly, if defensively. "Not a love child. We just didn't plan for this."

"Were you married to this woman before you, uh, copulated?"

I hesitated again. Fuck. "Why are you so hung up on my marriage?"

"So it *is* a love child?"

In a different frame of mind, under different circumstances — preferably in temperatures not hot enough to fry an egg on my head — I would have rebut her claim again. But I lacked the energy, and the fucking sun was showing its full strength.

"Let me have one of those cigarettes," I said.

She lifted one and handed it to me along with her lighter. "You okay there, Mikey?"

"Yeah, I'm fine, just don't tell my wife. I told her I quit."

"You see that? That is why marriage is fucked."

"What are you talking about?"

"You have to lie to your wife about smoking. What's the use in being married to a person if you have to lie about something as petty as smoking a cigarette?"

"In fairness, the last time I had a cigarette was when she left me at the altar. Since then I—"

"She left you at the altar? And you married this chick?"

"Well, I sort of left her at the altar too . . ."

Constance looked at me skeptically.

"It's long story, but my point is I don't lie to her all the time."

"All the time? What kind of a husband are you? No wonder you're spooked about having kids. You're still a kid yourself."

The truth of those words hit me in the mouth so hard, I found myself checking my lower lip for blood. Constance must have known she had hurt me.

"Look, I didn't mean to hurt your feelings. I just—"

"Don't worry about it," I said. "It's fine. I'm fine. I'm gonna go check on my phone. It's probably at least half-charged by now." I sauntered into the office. Cindy was nowhere in sight — Thank God — and my phone was nearly fully charged. I checked and saw I had three texts and eleven voicemails. The texts were from my brother, Fiona and my mother, and all of them were composed in shorthand, asking where I was. Then, I went onto the voicemails. I didn't make it halfway through the first one before I closed the phone and careered out of the door to find Constance.

"You have to get me to Norman Regional," I said.

"Why? What's wrong?"

"She's going into labor. You have to take me to the hospital."

FIVE

We jumped into the wrecker and took off toward the hospital. I was calling my brother and mother, and trying to explain the situation to Constance in between calls.

"So, you're about to be a daddy?" she said.

"No, it's my sister, Fiona."

I dialed Ron's number again, and thankfully, he answered his phone. "Where the hell have you been? We've been trying to reach you all day."

"It's a long story. How's Fiona?"

"She's on the table now. She's been asking for you. You need to get here now."

"I'm working on it."

"Mom is pissed at you and dad—"

"I said I'm on my way, Ron."

"Fine, just get here. I'll meet you at the east entrance." Ron hung up the phone.

"Is everything all right," Constance asked.

"Yeah," I said. "It's just, you know, dysfunctional family dynamics."

"Dysfunctional?"

"But, somehow, we function. Crazy, I know."

We pulled into the entrance under the hospital's brick awning and jumped out of the car. My brother was waiting for us in the sliding door entrance.

"Are you going to just leave your rig there?" I asked Constance.

"What are they gonna do?" Tow it?"

Good point.

My brother confronted me as soon as I was within shouting distance. "Come on," Ron said, gesturing for us to follow him.

"They took her into the operating room a couple of hours ago. Mom, Dad and June are waiting for us."

We followed him to the elevator, where I continued the conversation.

"Has anyone heard from her boyfriend?" I asked.

"No, you were always closest to her. We figured she would have given him your number. We were hoping he called you."

"He hasn't." I had checked the rest of my voice messages on the way to the hospital. Most were from my mom, who was hysterical, three were from Ron, and one was from June.

"What's she doing here?" Ron said, pointing a finger at Constance.

"She's my ride."

"But she's the stripper from Chesty's."

"And you're an asshole," Constance said.

Ron turned back to me. "You can't bring a stripper up here. What if June sees her?"

"Will you shut up about Constance? She saved my ass today — twice — and she's coming. Besides, we're the only people who knows she's a . . . a dancer."

See what I did there?

Ron shook his head and threw up his hands. "I'm warning you, if she finds out you were driven here by a stripper, she's liable to have a fucking miscarriage right there on the floor."

I shrugged him off and gave an apologetic look to Constance, but it didn't take. We marched off the elevator in single file with Ron leading the way. My mother, father and June were camped out in the hallway. My mother and June held hands while my father paced back and forth.

"I found him!" Ron called out, as if I had been lost in the Bermuda Triangle for decades.

My mother was the first to descend upon me. A tight hug was followed quickly by a swift open hand to the cheek. "Shame on you Michael Martin McNulty. Shame on you for making this family worry about you while your sister labors away in pain."

"What did I do?" And I was given another smack for my trouble.

"Your wife and I have been worried sick about you," my mother said, pointing at June.

June rose and walked over to me. This was awkward for several reasons, not the least of which was because A) I hadn't said more than three words to June in the past three days. B) She didn't greet me with a kiss or a hug. C) Constance stood just a few feet behind me, and God knows what she must have thought.

"We need to talk," June said.

"Yeah, I know," I said. "I haven't been dealing with . . . us the way I should be. I'm sorry about that." I went to hug her, but she pulled back. It took me a moment to understand why, and then I saw her eyes locked on Constance. I turned around, and saw that Constance was holding her gaze. Then, I felt my ass cheeks clinch, and reached into my pocket for my rosary. But as it turns out, I there weren't enough Hailmarys in the world.

June pulled her eyes back to me. "Did you sleep with her?" she asked.

Oh, fuck.

"No, of course not," I said. "She just gave me a ride here. It's a long story, but my car is in the shop because, it's . . . uh . . . broken. And—"

"I know what that bitch does for a living. But you didn't have to throw us away, throw this away for a perky pair of tits and ass."

"Bitch?" Constance said. "Who are you calling a bitch?"

"You, heifer."

"Heifer? You're the pregnant cow here."

That silenced the hallway. "You told her I was pregnant?" June said. "Your mother doesn't even know yet. My mother doesn't even know yet."

"She does now," Ron said.

On cue, my mother collapsed onto the floor. My father made a move for the first time since my arrival to try to help my mom. Ron went flying down the hall to get a doctor, and Constance went with him. June looked at me. Tears started welling up in her eyes. She made for the elevator. I ran after her and caught her at the elevator.

"June wait," I said. "Can't we just talk about this?"

"There's nothing to talk about," June said. "I came here to tell you I'm getting it taken care of."

"What? What are you talking about?"

She looked up at me through sad sobbing eyes. "I'm having an abortion. Don't come home tonight." The elevator door closed in front of me. I stood awestruck. I didn't know what I was supposed to do, or how I was supposed to do it. I turned around and walked back to where my mother was lying down. Ron and Constance had found a doctor, and he was attending to my mother on the ground. I bent down and asked how my mother was doing. She wasn't conscious. The doctor didn't have a chance to speak.

"This is your fault," my father shouted at me. His eyes were angry and rage had taken over his face. "If you hadn't gone and married that woman, that, that *nig*ger, none of this would have happened. You are no longer my son. I am no longer your father. You're dead to me."

"Dad?"

He didn't look up at me. He stared at my mom, brushed her hair and watched the doctor work.

"Dad," Ron said.

"Be quiet, Ronald," my father said.

I turned to Ron. His weak eyes and sullen face told me what he hadn't wanted to at Chesty's. I turned from him to Constance. She couldn't look me in the eye.

A nurse came through the double doors at the end of the hall. She was fully dressed in scrubs and looked anxious. "Is there a Mikey McNulty here?" she said.

I rose up. "That's me."

"Could you come with me? Your sister is asking for you."

I gave one more look to my unconscious mother, then to my father and followed the nurse back through the double doors.

My sister was waiting for me in bed, watching TV when I arrived. The nurse left us in the room alone.

"How are you feeling?" I said.

Fiona didn't take her eyes away from the television. "I feel like another human being forcefully removed himself from my body through a ten centimeter gap that used to be my vagina, but other than that I feel fine."

Amazing. Leave it to my baby sister to come through hours of child-bearing pain and come out the other side talkative and vibrant. She looked just as brilliant as she had the last time I saw her and had admittedly lost five to ten pounds of newborn from her waistline. Through the covers she looked just as small and frail as she always had.

I put my hands in my pockets and walked closer to her. "Do you need anything? Ice chips or something?"

"What I need is for this hospital to unclench its fiscal ass cheeks and invest in some premium cable. These channels suck. I mean, what kind of cable provider doesn't have ESPN?" She dropped the remote on the bed next to her and turned her attention to me. "Hey, what's wrong with you?"

I took a step back and fell into a nearby seat next to her bed. "Nothing, I'm fine. You called for me, so what's up?"

"You first. I haven't seen you look like this since dad shot Solomon in the backyard."

"He was a good dog. Dad should have never shot him."

"Solomon snapped at dad, Mikey."

"He was a puppy, and he was only trying to protect me from another beating. He would have done the same for you if he was your dog."

"Still, what did you expect to happen? Dad was always looking for away to get rid of him. Since the day mom let you bring Solomon home, Dad had it out for him."

"Well, he got rid of him, didn't he?" I said, sinking into the chair.

Fiona studied me for a moment. She always had a way of sizing me up with her big green eyes. I felt like an open book written in large bold print whenever I was with her. But that was part of what made us so close. She knew me, and I knew her.

"What did dad do, Mikey?" Fiona said in her authoritative motherly tone. She had that tone down since about age 12. I felt sorry for her kid. It was already outmatched and outgunned.

"Nothing," I said, feigning normalcy.

"Mikey, I have just born a child. Believe it or not, I am just a tad bit exhausted. So please be a good big brother, just this once, and tell me what happened."

Okay, but remember, she asked for it. So I told her — all of it. My car, Dad, Constance, Mom, June — she heard it all. And I will always love her for what she said next.

"You want me to have the nurses bring you up Guinness?"

I laughed. "You aren't worried about mom?"

"That woman will outlive us all. You know how she faints at the slightest bit of excitement. Answer my question."

"This is a hospital. You can't drink Guinness in a hospital."

"The hell you say." Fiona pushed a little red button connected to the intercom above her bed. "Watch this."

Less than a minute later a candy-striper appeared in the doorway. "Yes, Ms. McNulty."

"I'd like a pint of Guinness Draught, please. No glass — just bring me the bottle."

"I'm sorry, Ms. McNulty, but I can't allow you to have alcohol on the premises," the candy-striper said.

Fiona broke out in tears. She started sobbing loudly, and tossing around a cup of ice next to her bed, along with her pillows and the little red button she had used to summon the nurse. "Why can't you people just give me what I *want*? For Christ's sake, I've just given birth in this godforsaken shithole, and no one is willing to get me what I want. All I want is a pint of the black stuff. Is that too fucking *much* to ask?"

The candy-striper ducked yet another onslaught of flying debris and conceded. "I'll be right back. Please don't hurt me." The candy-striper took off out of the room at a run, probably never to be heard or seen at Norman Regional again.

"Was that completely necessary?"

"No," Fiona said, "but it was fun. You're one to talk anyway. I learned curse words from you — you fucking sailor."

Okay, fair enough.

"And the rest?" I said.

"Well, let's see. I learned the throwing and yelling part from mom. I learned all about Guinness from dad, and I learned to bitch about my current plight in life from our mutual older brother. See, you all have contributed greatly to my education."

Damn, that about sums up my family, now doesn't it? Lots of harsh truths were just being vaulted at me, and it was starting to feel a touch unfair. Shit, that sounds just like my brother. Right about now, my mother would tell me I should be more like Enoch. Enoch was a kiss-ass.

"So what did you ask me here for?" I said. "You know the rest of them will want to see you."

"Yeah, I'm sure mom and dad can't wait to see their mixed grandchild." My sister, she doesn't lack sarcasm.

A nurse walked into the room, holding a bundle in a little blue blanket. She walked around the bed and handed the blanket and its contents to my sister. She smiled at me and left the room.

"This is why I wanted you here," she said.

I rose out of my chair and crept closer to the bed. I peeked into the blanket, and saw a beautiful baby boy fast asleep in my little sister's arms.

Fiona looked up at me. "You're an uncle, Mikey — Uncle Mikey."

"He's beautiful," I said. And he was. He had my sisters eyes and cheeks and a full head of curly light brown hair atop his head.

"Do you want to hold him?" she said.

"Me? No, I might drop him, and his head might come flying off his neck or something."

She laughed. "No, I always told you you would be a great father." She placed him in my arms. I cradled him against my chest. He awoke there and smiled at me. No tears, no crying, just a big smile.

"Besides," Fiona said, "You wouldn't drop your namesake, would you?"

I looked up at her, surprised. "What do you mean, namesake?"

"He's named after you, silly. His name is Michael, Michael Moran McNulty. I had to sneak Pappy's name in there somewhere, or mom would have had one of her hissy fits. I'm going to call him Mikey for short, like his uncle."

I held my nephew close, reveling in his smile. He felt good in my arms. I hoped I felt the same way to him.

"So what are you going to do about, you know, your life?" Fiona said.

And just like that, all my good vibrations were gone. I gave my nephew back to Fiona and sat back in the chair next to her bed. "Well, I'm open to suggestions," I said, holding my hands up in surrender.

My sister took out one of her breasts and inserted it into my nephew's open gourd. Yeah, that's definitely listed under Shit I Didn't Expect, Nor Wanted to See Today.

"I think you should at least hear June out," Fiona said. "She's been with you for this long. She must have her reasons for wanting the abortion, even though she knows this family is too Catholic for its own good sometimes."

"Maybe you didn't hear me the first time," I said. "She told me not to come home."

"Yeah, and it's like I've told you before. Women just want to know you love us. We'll push you away as often as we need to in order to give you an opportunity to reaffirm your love."

"Okay, what about Constance?"

"You didn't sleep with her, did you?"

"No, I didn't."

"Then you'll have to do your best to explain that to June, maybe even with Constance's help, and see if you can't get to the root of why she wants to give up the baby."

"And Constance?"

"You'll just have to explain to her this how our family rolls. We're hysterical, loud, drunks, opinionated and fighters. If she's as good a person as you think she is, she'll understand. Dad is what's going to be the tough sell. Did he really say he disowned you?"

"'You are dead to me' were his exact words if I remember correctly." And I did.

"Fuck."

"Tell me about it."

"What do you think sent him over the edge?"

"God knows. First he didn't like that I married June. Then mom probably told him we got married without him. Now he's blaming me for mom passing out."

"Mikey the scapegoat."

"What?"

"Mikey the scapegoat — that's what Ron and I called you. It didn't matter what we did wrong, if we blamed it on you, we were fine."

"Really?"

"Remember when you got beat for breaking mom and dad's bedroom window with that basketball?"

"I didn't even like basketball."

"Sorry."

"It was you?"

"Yeah, but I didn't know dad would beat you the way he did. That's when I realized how much he doesn't like you for whatever reason."

"The old man hates me."

"Yeah, maybe, but you've still got to try to find out why, and then make it right."

"Why? Why should I?"

"He's your father, Mikey. And I know you hate him. God knows he hasn't done you any favors. But you only get one father in this life, and that's if you're lucky. I mean, look at my son. He's going to have to depend on his uncle to teach him a lot about what it is to be a man in this world."

"Ron is going to do a shitty job of that."

Fiona laughed. "Not Ron — you. You didn't think my son was going to bear your name while you sit on the sidelines, did you? No, buster, you're not getting off that easily." She smiled. My sister always had more faith in me than she should have, or at least I thought she should have. I loved her for that. I smiled back at her.

"I don't hate dad," I said. "I just really, really don't like him sometimes. He's the one who hates me."

"Promise me you'll try to work things out with him, preferably before the picnic, but for now, just promise me you'll try."

Why would I make a promise I had no fucking intention of keeping? Why would I go out of my way to try to rebuild a relationship that has been fractured since birth but was compounded not even an hour ago? I love my sister. That's why. Fuck me, I wish I didn't.

"I'll talk to him," I said.

"Before the picnic?"

"Don't push it, Fiona. Now what am I going to do about my car?"

"Find out what it will cost to fix it, and pay it."

"And if I can't?"

"Ride the bus. Now go get the rest of them. I'm sure by now mom is fine and chomping at the bit to bombard us with kisses and hugs."

SIX

I left my sister in her room with my nephew and went back the way I came, looking for my family. Ron and Constance were all that were left. Ron had just hung up the phone when he saw me coming.

"How is she?" Ron asked.

"She's fine. She must still be heavily medicated, too, because you would never know she had just given birth."

"That's good," he said. "And the baby?"

"The baby is fine, too. It's a boy."

"Mary-Katherine will be glad to hear that. I just got off the phone with her. She's on her way and bringing the rugrats with her. They'll be staying through the picnic with me, so after I see Fiona I'm going to have to get a bigger room at the Embassy Suites."

"The more the merrier."

"That's easy for you to say. You don't know what it's like to be married for years and wish for your freedom the way a man with a life sentence wishes for his."

"After today, I'll be lucky if my marriage makes it to the picnic."

"Oh. Yeah. Sorry, I forgot. That just happened, didn't it?"

"It did. I was kind of wishing I dreamt the whole thing, but now I have you to thank for grounding me in the piss-poor reality that is my life. Thank you, big brother."

"I said I was sorry."

"Yeah, yeah, where are mom and dad?"

"They're in the emergency room, getting mom checked out. She's fine. She came to almost as soon as you left. I guess that wasn't the best way for her to find out you two are pregnant. But at least I wasn't the one to tell her."

Constance sat on a bench near us. She shook her head at my brother's insensitivity.

"Well, she was bound to find out sooner or later," I said.

"But later would have been better," Ron said. My brother was being as empathetic as a hungry lion running down a baby antelope. "Do you really think June meant what she said about, you know," he leaned in to whisper the words, "getting an abortion."

"How should I know?"

"You *are* her husband."

Good point.

"Well, I don't know, Ron. I wish I knew she was joking, but I don't."

"Do you want to tell mom and dad that Fiona wants to see us?"

"No, that had better be you."

"All right, but you know mom is not done with this, right?"

"Right now, I'm not really worried about what I'm going to do about her."

"Yeah dad is . . . dad never really liked you as much."

See that, there? That's an open statement left to interpretation. As much as what? As much as another hole in the head? As much as being raped by a syphilitic Yeti?

"You and Fiona both, huh?"

"What?"

"Nothing. I'll deal with the dad later. Why don't you go get mom and dad and go visit our sister and nephew."

Ron cracked a smile and hugged me. "I hope you can patch this up with June," he said. "I know how much you love her. But if not, remember *I* told you she is an evil cunt." He pulled back and left down the hall. I just had to shake my head.

I sat down on the bench next to Constance. She perked her head up, and looked at me.

"I'm sorry about earlier," I said. "It just kind of came out."

"All can be forgiven if you will tell me what's going on between you and June, and why exactly she thinks I slept with you," Constance said.

"What would give you the impression I know anything about this at all?"

"You're her husband."

That was the second time in less than two minutes that I was reminded of that fact.

"Yes, I am," I said. "Are you implying there is something you know about my wife that I should know?"

Constance looked at me hard, but her eyes were tender. There was clearly something she wasn't telling me. "I don't want to talk about this," she said. "I'm going back to the garage. I have work to do." She stood up from the bench and began walking down the hall toward the elevator. I took off after her and stepped into the elevator with her.

"Wait, we need to talk about this," I said. "I want to talk about this."

"Fat people want to be slim. Short people want to be tall. Guess what? They're not getting what they want either."

"C'mon, Constance, you've got to talk to me."

She pressed the first floor button. "Talk to your wife."

"You saw her. She doesn't want to talk to me."

"What a coincidence; neither do I. Now shut up about it before you lose your ride back to the shop." Constance folded her arms and leaned against the elevator.

In that moment, I felt emasculated. My nuts, my balls, my marbles, my dice — they were no longer mine. They were the property of a timeshare between my wife, sister, mother and a stripper-mechanic I barely knew. God is a spiteful bitch.

We came to the lobby and found two security guards standing in front of Constance's wrecker: Big and Bigger. She stepped toward Big and Bigger, who were standing in front of the rig. She chose to politely address Bigger.

"Look, you can either move now, or I will move you," Constance said.

The security guard puffed out his oversized chest. "I'm sorry, ma'am, but I can't allow you to leave the premises. Your truck has been illegally parked here for well over an hour. You have to wait here until the police arrive."

"Fine, have it your way." She took one step back, then kicked Bigger dead center in his crotch with her steel toe. He fell to his knees, hands covering his manhood with tears filling his eyes. Rather than try his luck, Big moved out of the rig's way.

Constance turned to me. "Are you coming?"

I nodded and stepped into the truck. "Are you okay?" I asked.

"Yes," Constance said. "I'm fine. That security guard was just in the wrong place at the wrong time."

"Do you want to talk about it?"

"No, I just want to do that to my ex-husband," she said, starting the car and pulling out of the hospital's brick awning.

"Ex-husband?"

She turned to me, her eyes afire this time. "I don't want to talk about him either."

This time I didn't have to be reminded to keep my hands to myself. I put my hands on my lap — over my crotch to be exact — and kept my mouth shut for the duration of the ride back to Earl's.

The ride back to the garage seemed to take less time than the ride to the hospital, but I wasn't complaining. I jumped out of the rig as soon Constance came to a stop.

"I'll go check with Earl and see about your car," Constance said. "You should probably go check-in with Cindy. I'll come get you when I know something."

Ah, the Justin Bieber devil child.

"Okay, I'll go see if she has yet another mountain of paperwork for me to fill out."

Sure enough when I walked into Earl's blank white office, Cindy was leaned over the same magazine she was the first time I walked in. She had since added a piece of bubble gum to the mix and was now blowing bubbles as large as her head, popping them on her chin and sucking the excess back into her mouth like a vacuum cleaner.

I waved my hand in between her face and the magazine. She popped her head up. The Children of the Corn could learn a thing or two from her lethal gaze. She pulled out one of her headphones. "What?" she said, as she masticated her bubble gum like an overfed cow. And we say the youth of today have no couth.

"I'm just here checking on my car?"

"Earl's got it in the back," she said.

"You wouldn't happen to know what's wrong with it, would you?"

"You'll have to ask Earl."

"Did he mention how much whatever is wrong with the car is going to cost?"

"You'll have to ask Earl."

"Right. Ask Earl." I turned away, defeated by a teenage girl. No one will ever accuse me of being a ladies' man. I sat down in the same chair I had once before and waited for something to happen. I pulled out my phone to see if I had any messages or missed phone calls. I hadn't had any. I thought about Fiona and my nephew. What had possessed her to name her son after me was beyond me. I wouldn't have named my *own* child after me. I hadn't done anything worthwhile. There were plenty of other men — smart strong men — she could have named him after. Why not name him after Alexander the Great? He was a great conqueror and leader. Why not name him after Saint Augustine? Much of his work has helped mold the way we westerners think about Christians and Catholicism. On second thought, that might not be the best name for a kid after all. Why not name him after Tupac? He was probably the greatest lyricist this world will ever know. A kid of Irish descent in Oklahoma with the name Tupac Amaru Shakur McNulty. Yeah, that would have drove my parents crazy. I guess it wouldn't have been as bad if she had named him after the Archangel, but she hadn't. She had named him after me.

"Mikey," Constance said. "Hey, Mikey are you in there?"

"Yeah," I said, snapping back to reality. "I was just thinking about Tupac."

"The rapper?"

"Yeah, the rapper."

"You do realize you're white with the last name McNulty, right?"

Reality check.

"Yes, yes I do," I said.

"Anyway, Earl is ready to give you the damage report on your car?"

"Damage report?"

"His words, not mine."

Fuck all.

"Lead the way."

I followed Constance outside to the garage bay where my car sat with the hood up. She left me in front of my car and headed over to the rig. Leaning against the hood of my car wiping, his filthy hands on a filthy rag was a short, plump black man. He had on coveralls, a "Sooner Football 4Ever" hat and a cigarette in the curve of his lip. He reached out his hand, and I shook it, choosing not to wipe the grease off my palm right away. In some countries, such a gesture might be viewed as an insult, and Earl's garage was most definitely his country.

"Earl Pearl," he said boisterously. "Good to meet 'cha."

"Likewise, Mr. Pearl," I said.

"Oh, no, don't call me mister. I work for a living."

"I prefer the formality, Mr. Pearl. I was raised to respect my elders."

Earl nodded his head and smiled. "Bob was right about you. I'm not usually one to like you white boys, but Bob and I go way back. If he says you good people, you good people," he said, taking my hand again and shaking it with both of his this time.

"Thank you," I said. "Bob?"

"Bob Summers — your daddy-in-law. You're June's husband, ain't 'cha?"

"Oh, yeah, of course I am."

He nodded his head demonstratively. "Oh, good, good. Like I said, the rest of us weren't sold when we found out June runoff with some white boy from across the tracks. You know, without her mama and daddy and the rest of us folks who helped raise that little girl in attendance. But Bob, he always spoke highly of you. So I'll give you the benefit of the doubt."

"I appreciate that, sir."

"No problem, white boy. Is this here your vehicle?"

"Yes, sir. It is."

"Oh, I'm sorry to hear that — it's a real piece of shit."

See? Told you.

"Is there anything you can do to fix that?"

"Earl can fix anything on wheels and most things that ain't."

Did he just refer to himself in the third person?

"So how much is this going to cost me?"

"Oh, I'd say about ten Gs ought to do it."

"Ten *thousand* dollars?"

"I like the way Earl said it better to be honest with you, but have it your way. The customer is always right in Earl's shop."

Christ, make it stop.

"I don't have that kind of money," I said.

I omitted "ever" from the end of that sentence.

"Earl's sorry to hear that. I can have Constance tow your car to your residence for one hundred and forty-nine dollars and ninety-five cents plus gas."

Fuck.

"Let me think about."

"Don't think too long. It's about quitting time for Earl."

I walked over to Constance, who was smoking another cigarette by the rig and told her about my car. "Sucks to be you," she said.

You have no idea.

"Do you think you can talk to him for me?"

"And tell him what?"

"Just get him to let me leave the car here for a week or so while I try to figure something out."

"I can try, but this would be a lot easier if you had money to give him."

"Trust me, if I had any, it would be in his hands right now. Just do this for me, please."

She put out her cigarette and spoke to Earl. I watched as they gabbed back and forth for a few minutes. Both of them were using their hands to talk, which meant Constance was at least putting up a fight for me. Their conversation came to an end with Earl storming off into the garage. Constance walked back over to me and put her hands on her hips.

"He's not going to let you leave your car here."

"Why the hell not? People leave their cars at automotive garages all the time while they're being worked on."

"True, but most of those people can pay for the parts and labor being performed on said cars. You made the mistake of admitting to Earl you don't have the money to pay him. Besides, his mediocre skills as a mechanic don't pay the bills around here. My repo skills do, and we need the space for cars I'll be towing in and out of here. But he is going to let me tow your car to your house free of charge."

"I don't have a house. I live in an apartment village."

"Well, there's plenty of parking there then. Do you want me to tow the car or not?"

I sighed. "Okay, it doesn't sound like I have a choice."

Constance nodded her head and got into the rig. I followed. She started it up and faced me. "Look, after I drop your car off, I'll buy you a drink. Sound good?"

"You don't have to work tonight?"

"No, I'm off. Even Women of the Pole need time off."

"One drink isn't gonna fix this."

"Fine, I'll buy you more than one drink. Just promise not to pass out."

"I can hold my liquor," were my famous last words.

SEVEN

I guided Constance to my apartment village, and she put my car into an empty space. I looked around for June's car, but I didn't see it. She was at her parent's house, I supposed. Constance climbed back into the cab of the rig.

"Are you ready to go?" she said.

"Yeah, where are we going? Maguires?"

"No, we're not going anywhere near that high-and-mighty pitiful excuse for a bar. We're going to a *real* tavern."

My whole life is a lie.

"Anywhere I know?"

"You ever been to Sack and Balls?"

There were many stories floating around about guys and girls who disappeared in the middle of a semester after claiming they were going out to Sack and Balls. So no, I had never been to Sack and Balls for that reason and many others, not the least of which is the patrons and owner's reputation for disposing of any unwelcome clientele into a nearby ditch that was rumored to house hundreds of dismembered limbs from the bodies of the most misguided and fool-hearted of yokels and college kids. You might say it was like a frat house, except if you didn't pass the initiation you were never heard from again. Ever. Forgive me for being such a pussy in my college days, but for some reason I seemed to value life, even with the knowledge that my degree mandated, at some point, that I would have to think about suicide. Being that I'm Catholic — as you know doubt have a firm grasp of by now — that last part never sat well with me. I mean, would you waste all these God points you've earned over the past twenty-three years just to hang from a short rope at the end of a ceiling fan, soiled in your own feces and be condemned to an eternity of damnation and torture at the hands of some fallen angel? I think not.

"Nope," I said, "I've never been there. I guess tonight is as good a night as any."

I omitted, "to die" from the end of that sentence.

"Good, that means Buford doesn't know you," Constance said.

"Who's Buford?"

"Buford is the owner and barkeep at Sack and Balls. If he doesn't like you, you don't get in."

Or out, if the legends are true.

"Don't worry," Constance said. "Buford is all right. You just have to know how to talk to him."

"And you know how to talk to him?"

"I do."

Constance pulled the rig into a packed parking lot — or I guess I should keep it literal and say "a packed, previously-empty-and-void-of-any-sort-of-vegetation dirt lot" — filled with trucks. There were semis, diesels, trucks that said Cummins on the back, trucks with owners who weren't shy about their truck's 4x4 capabilities, trucks with ladders in the back of them, trucks with bales of hay in the back of them, trucks with mud flaps, trucks that *looked* like mud flaps, and three other trucks outfitted for towing. Suffice to say, there were a lot of trucks in this parking lot. We jumped out of the truck, and I fell in line behind Constance, hoping her presence would ward off any evil body-dismembering bandits that may or may not inhabit Sack and Balls.

"Are you okay?" Constance said, looking back at me.

"Sure, I'm fine. I just don't want to lose you in this maze."

"What maze? There are two pool tables, a juke box and a bar. What are you going to get lost in?"

To be fair, she left out the eight sets of tables and chairs — yes, I counted — the dartboard and the pay phone up against the wall.

We sat near the center of the bar, and Constance ordered us two shots and two beers. "Jack Daniels straight up and a Boulevard Wheat?" she said.

"Yeah, a change of pace would be nice," I said.

"Change of pace?"

"Yeah, the beer; I've been drinking Guinness since I was 12."

"Since you were 12, huh? They have laws against that."

"Yeah, well, my Pappy thought I should start early."

"It's a wonder you're not an alcoholic."

"I usually only drink around my family."

"I'd want to drink around them too, especially your mother. She's a bit high-strung."

"She means well."

Our shots and beers arrived along with a robust man with a tattoo around his neck that looked like it used to be barbed wire, but was now just splotchy saggy ink. "Who's the squirrel?" he said to Constance.

"Buford, this is Mikey. Mikey, this is Buford Brooks."

I reached out to shake Buford's hand, but he just left his two oven mitts on the bar. I put my hand in my pocket. "Brooks, that's an interesting name. Any relation to Garth Brooks?"

Buford didn't smile. He didn't move. In fact, I think he may have growled at me. "The squirrel's with you, Connie?" he said to Constance.

"Yep," she said.

Buford grumbled under his breath — something about "those damn college kids" — and left us to pour someone else a drink.

"He's a charmer," I said.

"You didn't do yourself any favors with that Garth Brooks quip."

"What quip? I asked the man a question."

"Would you have asked him the same question if you weren't in this bar and his first name wasn't Buford?"

Fuck no.

"Perhaps," I said. "We will never know." I drank my shot and chased it with a sip of beer. It turns out, all brands of whiskey have the same flavor — hellfire. I coughed and wheezed at the bar and slurped down more beer.

"I thought you said you'd been drinking since you were 12?"

I coughed once more. "What I meant to say is I had my first drink when I was 12."

"What about drinking around your family?"

"I don't like to drink around them. They drink enough for me, anyway. Two pints of Guinness, and I'm usually through."

Constance shook her head and laughed. I watched her throw back her drink without so much as nervous tingle. "Why would a guy like you want to get married?"

"No, no more talk about me. Why would a girl like you want to get married?"

She sipped her beer and turned on me in her stool. "I told you I don't want to talk about it."

"I do want to talk about it, and I'm the one with the bigger problems."

"Tough shit."

"I won't talk to you anymore until you tell me about your marriage."

"Then I guess we won't talk."

We sat, speechless, next to each other for the next ten minutes, nursing our beers. I can't tell you how hard it was to keep my mouth closed. I mean, I like talking for the most part. I counted the number of bald bearded men in the bar. I played I Spy with myself and searched for tramp stamps on women. I even tried to find a pair shoes that weren't steel toes or cowboy boots in a kind of

Where's Waldo fashion. Then, just when I was about to try to count the number of cigarette butts in the bar, Constance spoke.

"He's five-ten with bushy brown hair and an asshole," she said.

"Who is?"

"My ex-husband."

"So I take you aren't on speaking terms?"

Dumb question, but one I thought was perfectly valid at the time.

"No, we're not."

"What happened?"

"I was young and stupid. That's what happened."

"How old are you now? You said you were young and stupid. I just wonder how old you are now?"

"Not that it's any of your business, but I'm 21."

"How old were you when you got married?"

"I was a freshman at that fucked up university, so 18 and change."

"Wait, back up. I thought you said you never went to OU?"

"No, I said wasn't going there now — kind of like you and your history of drinking, right?"

I asked for that.

"Okay, how long did it last?"

"About as long as the courtship. He told me he loved me. I was stupid enough to believe him. He could afford to fly both of us to Vegas, where, naturally, we eloped. Six months later he filed for divorce. After that, I threw away my scholarship and learned to repossess what doesn't belong to me. Stripping came later. You know that asshole even tried to say he was sorry the other day? But it doesn't matter now. I've saved up enough money to do what I originally came here to do anyway."

"What's that?"

"I want to teach modern dance and be a choreographer in San Diego."

"Like Martha Graham?"

"What do you know about Martha Graham?"

"Hey, I took A History of Dance during sophomore year. They don't give the Presidential Medal of Freedom to just anyone, except I think she danced in New York."

Constance smiled and ordered us two more shots, and that one burned just as much as the first one. I was starting a feel a little tipsy.

"Well, I don't have to be as famous as her," she said. She threw back another shot. "It's a dream I've been working toward, you know?"

Constance pulled back and finished the rest of her beer. "You look like you have something else you want to ask me," she said.

"Forgive me for being selfish, but where does June fit into all of this?"

Constance sighed and sat back in her stool. "My ex-husband and I met outside of Catlett, you know, the music hall. I was majoring in dance, and he was majoring in Finance. He was older, much older. Anyway, some of the girls I had class with found out — probably from him now that I think about it — that I had sex with him. One of those girls was June. Not for nothing, but did you have to marry her? She's a great dancer, but I wouldn't marry her."

She ordered two more shots, and I was feeling more than a little tipsy. Look, I'm not as much of a lightweight as I seem to be. I just hadn't had anything to eat in awhile. You try keeping all that liquor from hitting you while on an empty stomach. See if you don't feel a little less than sober.

"Thanks for bashing my wife's character. I will always cherish this moment."

"I'm sorry. It's just that she's always been a little out there."

"Again with the bashing?"

"Fine, I'll stop. But you wanted to know where she fits in, and I'm telling you. Now about you: Do you like being a reporter?"

"What's not to like?"

Constance squinted at me.

"The hours suck and my boss hates me, but it's a job. There are worst jobs in the world. My family comes from working with their hands. My siblings and I are the first to rage against the machine and get jobs that don't require us to sweat profusely or form calluses out of necessity."

"What would you do otherwise? You know, if you weren't working a job where the hours suck and your boss hates you?"

"I'd be writing novels. I'd be a novelist." The words just came out all on their own. I didn't even need to think about it. I wanted to write novels.

"What kind of novels? You look like a J.R.R. Tolkien or George R.R. Martin kind of dork? I'm sure you've read a lot of *some*thing that has 'R.R.' attached to it."

"Maybe." I hate it when they can just read you blind like that. It's like a vaginal superpower or something.

"Okay, so who are some of your other favorite writers?"

"Nick Hornby, Billy Shakespeare, Christopher Moore, Elmore Leonard, Jane Austen, Cormac McCarthy—"

"I loved All the Pretty Horses," Constance broke in. "And The Road? Best Sci-Fi book I've ever read."

Of all the names I did mention, I admit, that was the one I thought she was least likely to latch onto. I mean, look at that list and you can easily see the one that stands out from the rest.

"You know Cormac McCarthy?"

"Of course I do," Constance said. "What? You think just because I've got big boobs, blonde hair and great ass that I don't read good literature?"

"I'm sorry."

"Don't be. Most men think the same thing. And normally, I'd tear them a new asshole. But I like you."

"Thanks, I guess."

"No, you don't understand." Constance put her hand on my thigh and squeezed. "I really like you."

Bless me, Father for I have sinned. Again.

And then she kissed me.

I remember that much. I know I remember that. She kissed me with tongue and closed it out with her lips wrapped around my bottom lip in the middle of a smoky bar that smelled as much like cigarettes as it did musty armpits. But in that moment, I could have cared less. It felt good. But it's right after that point that I get a little hazy, that I miss some details. I wish I remembered it. I really do. It would have made what was to come next much more bearable.

Book Four:

Out Of The Fire

ONE

All right, before you judge me, you have to understand what I was dealing with. No matter what any man will tell you, there is nothing more tempting, coveted and chased than a beautiful woman. If beauty is in the eye of the beholder, all men are fucked.

Some chick named Delilah took down the strongest Israelite the world has ever known. Some chick called Jezebel killed enough Israelites to be remembered as the symbol for all fallen women, while convincing her husband — the motherfucking king of Israel — to change his *religion*. That's how good the nookie was. Some chick named Bathsheba seduced the leading scorer of the Old Testament All-Stars and one of God's all-time favorites in David, king of Judah, while the man was married and convinced him to send her then-husband into battle to die. Bathsheba gets points for giving birth to Solomon, but she's still a bad bitch.

Women are a supernatural force. I mean, they even have their own commandment: "Thou shalt not covet thy neighbor's wife . . ." Notice, He didn't put "thy neighbor's husband" in there. Why? Because He knew men are feeble creatures — made in His own image no less — with no hope to have any real dominion over the opposite sex. Sure, there is scripture that speaks to women being subordinate to men, but I'm beginning to think that is all a ruse. I mean, if we were truly meant to lead women, would God have made men so weak? Why I couldn't I have simply said, "No, Constance, I'm married. I shouldn't have sex with you because that wouldn't fix things. It would only serve to compound my problems. I think it's best that you take me home to my shitty apartment and leave me to sleep in front of my door because my wife will not be letting me in." But that's not what I said. Those weren't the words that came out of my mouth. I didn't hear God, Jesus, or even fucking Jiminy Cricket pleading with me to stop.

Why didn't I hear His great booming voice issuing me a grand warning from the likes of a concrete sky? Why didn't God reach down with His almighty hand and say, "Whoa there, my good son. Do you really want to knock boots with this woman? Here? Now? Shouldn't you be at home thinking of your unborn child?" I'll tell you why God didn't say anything to me: God is a spiteful bitch who gave birth to a spoiled — if once crucified — Son who will never let us fucking forget it, who I presumed to follow into the depths of the damned. Yeah, that's right — I followed Jesus straight to Hell. The difference between Jesus and yours truly: He was able to leave after just three days. I have been here for twenty-odd years. And apparently, Highway-9 leads not only to Purcell but straight to Hell. I know this because I woke up with a headache that felt as if John Henry was hammering away at my brain. My pants were around my ankles, and Constance was lying on my arm next to me. Her pants were off, but her shirt remained. I nudged her with a forceful poke in the shoulder to wake up. She slowly came to, and looked just as awful and disoriented as I felt.

"What the hell happened last night?" I said. "My head feels like it was crushed by the Goliath's ass."

"You promised you wouldn't pass out," Constance said. "Don't you remember?"

"I've got a pretty good idea about the big picture, but I'm more than a little fuzzy on the details."

Constance gestured to my pants, then to hers. "Do you need it drawn out in crayon? We fucked, okay? We were both drunk, and we made a mistake."

There it was: the truth as naked as the day I was born. Fuck.

I looked at my watch and saw it was just after six in the morning. And then an ominous feeling came over me. I've never liked having that feeling. It always foreshadowed my doom. It had shown up right before I bombed my ACT. It had shown up right before Roy Lee and his cronies jumped me in high school for talking to his girlfriend — a beating that left me hospitalized for several days, and it had shown up right before June had made that fateful phone call to call off our wedding.

"What day is today?" I said.

"I don't know," Constance said, pulling her pants on.

I gasped. "Today is tomorrow. Shit, shit, shit, shit — *shit*. You have to drive me to the Sentinel."

"What for?"

"So I can grovel to my boss that hates me, and hope he doesn't fire me."

We made our way out of a patch of high grass behind Sack and Balls and got into the rig. Constance took off down 12th avenue toward Main Street. I focused my eyes on the road, trying to think of what I was going to say to Marty. "Hey, Marty, I know you said have this story in by four o'clock, but you'll never believe what happened to me." Nope, that wouldn't work. How about, "Hey,

Marty, have you ever had a really bad day?" He would laugh in my face at that. "There is a perfectly logical explanation for why I don't have a story written, and why you shouldn't fire me."

I felt a punch in my shoulder. "Earth to Mikey," Constance said. She punched me in the shoulder again.

"Ouch," I said, "What the hell was that for?"

"Is it nice there in Lala Land?"

"What are you talking about?"

"You've been in a trance since we got in here. Hitting you was the only way I could get your attention."

"Well you've got it now. What do you want?"

"Don't you think we should talk about what happened last night?"

"Oh, now you want to talk? Okay, sure. I'll tell you what happened. You got me drunk and had sex with me to get back at my wife."

"Is that how you remember it?"

"Sure is."

I lied. For fuck's sake, I don't know why I lied. I was afraid, I guess. Stop asking me.

"You have a shitty memory," Constance said, hammering on the gears like they were a boxer's face.

Nope, I'm not even going to argue that point.

"Okay," I said, "What do you remember?"

She turned her eyes from the road, and sternly looked at me. "Nothing," she said. "I don't remember anything."

"That's not true; otherwise you wouldn't have brought it up."

"It's true now."

"You go to Hell for lying."

"I'll meet you there, asshole."

Constance made an unexpected and unscheduled stop off of 12th avenue in front of St. Mary.

"Oh, good, you read my mind," I said. "I have much to confess, and it's probably a good idea to go the Sentinel with a clear conscious."

"I'm not stopping for you. I have things of my own to discuss with my priest."

"You never told me you were Catholic?"

"You never asked." Constance jumped out of the rig and stormed toward the church. I got down from the rig and followed.

We both came to Father Jacob's office at the same time. "Ah, Constance, Michael," he said, "how good it is to see you both."

"I have come for confession, Father," Constance said.

"Me too. But I need to go first."

"My children," Father Jacob said, rising from his seat behind his desk. "I will take your confession in turn. Michael, I'm afraid I was raised to believe ladies should always go first."

"Father, this is no time for etiquette," I said. "I *really* need to confess to you."

"Yes, I can see you do. But I don't think the Rapture will occur before I have heard Constance's confession and then your own. Now, be still."

Be still. He might as well have used his most lethal spell of profanity and called me something so vile and demeaning that I would have wanted to dig myself a large hole and stay there for the rest of my natural born days. Be still is Father Jacob at his most sadistic.

Father Jacob showed us out of his office, into the sanctuary and directed me to sit in the first row of pews while Constance and he stepped into their respective sin bins. So there I was with just The Emaciated One above the altar to keep me company. I never liked being in a cathedral by myself, and I especially didn't like being in a cathedral by myself with a soul full of wickedness and filth while waiting to be cleansed and made whole again. I always felt like God was more likely to strike down the sinful in a cathedral than anywhere else. I mean, think about it. It takes some gall to enter God's house knowing you have probably broken eight of ten commandments (multiple times) within the past seventy-two hour window. I sat twiddling my thumbs for about two minutes before my hands found their way to my rosary beads. I lost count of the Hailmarys I prayed — because Our Father and Glory Be didn't seem appropriate, and as far as I knew, there was no novena for what I was dealing with — in the time Constance was in the sin bin with Father Jacob. I chose to keep my eyes shut, not out of reverence but out of fear. I knew The Emaciated One was staring down from his plastic painted cross at me. I did not want to provoke him. Something tells me if God had to choose between his only Son and Mikey McNulty, my ass was grass. My prayers were interrupted just twice. Each time I could have sworn it was someone crying.

Not long after I finished another Hailmary, Constance came out of her booth and took off at a jog toward the cathedral entrance. "Hey, you're going to wait for me, right?" I called out. She just kept running.

"I am ready for you, Michael," Father Jacob said, coming out of his booth.

"Where did she go, Father?" I said, pointing toward the door.

"I don't know, my son. Do you still want to confess?"

"Father, you have no idea how bad I want to confess."

I stepped into the door and revealed to Father Jacob all that had happened over the past twenty-four hours. He didn't interrupt me. He didn't try to tell me to calm down because I had to have been talking a mile-a-minute. He simply listened. There aren't enough people left in the world who simply listen. I always liked that about Father Jacob. When I was done, we both sat in silence for a few seconds until I couldn't stand it any longer.

"So what should I do?"

"I don't think these are the kind of problems that can be solved with a few prayers."

No, those are not the words you want to hear your priest utter — especially while he sits on the other side of the confessional booth. "Not for nothing, Father, but that doesn't really help me. I need advice in the absence of penance but would love to be punished too."

"Fiona has always been blessed with wisdom beyond her years, even if she doesn't always heed it herself."

"So you're saying I should go home and try to fix things with June—"

"And your father," he broke in. "Each of those relationships are key to you, whether you want them to be or not. Your willingness to fix one and not the other will leave you unbalanced and ill-equipped to handle relationships you haven't even considered."

"I like the man less and less since I married June, and there is no mistaking how he feels about me."

"Perhaps, but you should still try to talk to him. You should still try to repair that relationship. If not for your sake, then for the sake of your nephew, your sister and your ties to the rest of your family. It is very hard to live for God without a family's support."

"No offense to present company, Father, but God and I aren't vibing right now."

"God has a plan for us all."

"But what if that plan is to be a shit-heel for the rest of one's life?"

"Do you think God's plan for you is for you 'to be a shit-heel,' as you say?"

"Father, have you been listening at all?" I rarely got testy with Father Jacob, but I was starting to see him less as my priest in that moment and more like the uncle I wish I had.

"Yes, I have been listening. I know that you are frustrated with life. You have been frustrated for a long time. I also know that you took a leap of faith marrying June, but I know you were happy when you married her. I know that because I was the one who married you to her. Do you think I would have married the two of you if I didn't believe you loved her?"

"Honestly, Father, I never knew you had a say."

"Of course I do. I would never marry two people if I thought they did not love each other."

"So what now?"

"Now, you get out of this booth and tell your superior at the newspaper exactly what happened to you yesterday, omitting none of the details."

"Omitting none of the details?"

"Yes, the truth is always the best answer, the best explanation, the best cure for a tortured conscious."

"Forgive me, Father, but your idea sounds like the kind of total and uttered horseshit that will get me canned."

"Perhaps, but you will feel better about yourself and the way you handled this situation in the future if you simply tell the truth today. I am not promising you a happy ending, only a happier Michael McNulty."

We stepped out of our booths and hugged each other. It wasn't until after Father Jacob let me go and wished me well that I realized how much I loved and trusted him; not for being my priest but for being my friend. I really needed a friend then.

Outside of St. Mary's I looked for Constance and the rig, but neither were in the parking lot. In fact, there was no sign of Constance at all. She had left me there, and I couldn't blame her. She had clearly been upset earlier, and I should have known something was wrong when she asked me if I wanted to talk. But I was too absorbed in my own shit to even acknowledge that she probably just needed someone to talk to. Then again, she had obtained a friend, or at least I hoped she had, in Father Jacob. Then I remembered again that she left off in a hurry, sobbing from the confessional booth. I thought about going back into St. Mary to press Father Jacob about Constance one more time, but I thought better of it. I had to get started on my trek toward the Sentinel.

Walking from Porter to Main didn't take as much time as I thought it would, though I suspect it was hotter than the hinges of Hell on the day in question. The pit stains on my shirt ran the length of my waist. It helped that St. Mary's was only a few blocks north on Porter to Main. But walking Main during rush hour nearly got me killed. The one-way, two-lane road becomes a four-lane right at the corner of N. Peter and Main where the Norman Sentinel News building is located. Me, being the dumbass that I am and feeling pressed for time, I tried to jaywalk across four lanes of traffic, and ended up dodging two cars that I now feel should've plastered me against the pavement. I ended up simply walking to the crosswalk and waiting for the walk sign to formally give me the go-ahead. In retrospect, I probably would have had time to come up with something beautiful and witty to say to Marty at my desk if I had just gone straight to the crosswalk in the first place. As it was, I met him face to face at the double-doors that led to the newsroom. Fuck.

"Why you little shit," Marty said. "You've got to have a pair of balls on you the size of two steroidal cantaloupes to show your face at this newspaper."

He said it as if this newspaper was on par with the fucking Washington Post. No, sir, this newspaper's primary rival is the Oklahoma Register — weekly tabloid readers can pick up for free.

I closed my eyes, took a deep breath, and then looked up at Marty. In the next five to seven minutes, I opened up to Marty on a level I would have thought impossible for me to do with such a slimy, mustachioed pompous racist like him. I told him all about the day before, about actually reporting the story, if not writing it, about LaRon, about my car, about my sister, about my nephew and everything. I just knew, in that moment, I was following Father Jacob's advice. After all, he is a priest.

Marty took stock of me in the doorway. He played with his mustache for a few seconds and then adjusted his crotch. He sniffed, and said "You're fired." He pushed open the door to the newsroom and disappeared from view.

I stood momentarily stunned. I had thought it could happen. I even expected it at various points throughout the morning, but it was surreal when it happened. It was like seeing my own death minutes before the freight train actually hit me, crushing my body and scattering my limbs into the brush. I didn't immediately understand, so I did something out of character: I stormed into the newsroom, looking for Marty.

The rest of the staff was looking at me, and judging from their faces, they all must have thought I was missing a few screws. Some of them made for the newsroom door. Others just gawked at me as I passed them by. But all of them seemed scared — scared that behind my back I might be holding an AK-47, and I was about to go postal on the entire staff. But now that I think about it, I wasn't as angry as some of them might have thought. I simply wanted answers.

I found Marty in the break room, rifling through the refrigerator, surely about to consume food that wasn't his. In my single-minded state, I tapped him on the shoulder and said, "Why?"

Marty popped up from the refrigerator, looking annoyed. "McNulty, I fired you. You don't work here anymore. Leave before I call security."

"I know you fired me. I simply want to know why."

Marty studied my face for a moment, and after seeing that I wasn't going anywhere, he closed the refrigerator. "I don't like you, McNulty. I don't like the way you go about your business in this newsroom. I don't like your flowery language in news stories. I don't like having to look at you every time I come to work. I don't like your choices in women. But mostly, I don't like that you think you can just not turn in a story assigned to you days ago and believe telling me you had bad day is a good enough reason for skipping out. I don't want you on my desk."

"Everyone else has just moved me to another desk," I protested.

"I don't like that either. I don't pass the buck, McNulty. You're not a newspaperman. You're a flighty squirrelly hack with no backbone. It's a wonder any woman thinks your man enough to marry, let alone some darkie."

And then it happened.

I know where it came from. I know why I did it. But I never expected myself to do it. I never expected myself to follow through with the thought, the emotion — the animalistic rage. But before I could take it all back, Marty was laid out on the break room floor, and I was standing over him with my fists still clinched. The newsroom staff gathered around to see what had happened, and it didn't take long for Chief Ellis to shoulder his way to the front of the crowd.

The chief looked at me, then at a stunned and bleeding Marty. "Marty, get up. You have work to do."

"But chief," Marty said, "he hit me."

"You'll live, won't you? Now get to work. Besides, I heard you and you're getting off light." The chief turned to me. "McNulty, follow me. We need to talk."

I nodded and followed the chief through the throng and out of the newsroom. He took me out back behind the Sentinel building. I knew the spot. We smokers gathered in it. The chief produced a pack of cigarettes and lighter from his shirt pocket. He offered me one. I took it and let the smoke fill my lungs. The chief gestured to a nearby bench, and we both took a seat on it.

"The bad news first: You are fired. But not for any of the reasons Marty mentioned, though I would never condone a reporter not filing a budgeted story for any reason. This is a bad time for newspapers. Everything is going to the Internet. News is tweeted, blogged and shared on Facebook hours before it makes it to a copy desk. We're . . . I'm being forced to cut back on my staff. Guys like Marty and Larry are unionized. You're one of newest reporters at the paper, and ordinarily that would mean we would try to keep you on at a pay cut. But I unknowingly screwed you when I promoted you to writing features and signed off on your raise. That put you in the crosshairs of the bean counters, and they think it makes more sense to cut a junior reporter than an old asshole like Marty. I'm sorry about that. But I do think Marty was right about one thing: You aren't a newspaperman. This isn't where you wanted to end up. I can read that in your copy; it's all adjectives and adverbs but gorgeously written stuff. I wish you did want to be a newspaperman, though. You are a helluva reporter. I just can't afford to pay you. The good news: We'll be able to give you a few months' severance, and you can have your benefits for six months."

I tried to let all that the chief said sink in, but most of it just skimmed the surface. I was in a deep dark hole, and in the last five minutes it had morphed into the Mariana Trench. I took a drag and said, "So what now?"

"That's for you to figure out. I can't help you with that. But if you need a letter of recommendation for your next job, just let Greta know, and I'll ship it out ASAP, okay?"

I nodded. "Can I collect my things, and make a phone call before I leave?"

"Sure," the chief said. "Take all the time you need." He crushed out his cigarette, patted me on the shoulder and left me on the bench.

I called my brother and he answered on the fourth ring. "What's up, little brother?" Ron said. "Have you talked to the wife yet?"

"Come pick me up," I said.

"Still haven't got your car out of the shop, huh?" He was laughing. That asshole was laughing at me.

"I don't want to talk on the phone. Just come pick me up."

"Fine, fine, where are you?"

I told him where I was, and he said he would be around to pick me up in a few minutes.

I didn't get it. I mean, I got it, but I still didn't get it. I was fired because I was young. No, I was fired because I was young and Marty couldn't stand me. Oh, fuck it. I was fired and that in itself was enough to go on a three-day bender in my family. The McNulty's never took news of layoffs, strikes or firings well, as my parents will vouch for. It's always been a staple of pride in my family that we hold down jobs. We find work doing something, somewhere, because we aren't too proud to do almost anything. For all of my parent's faults, living by that mantra always put food on the table for me and my siblings. We were never hungry; only tired and frustrated. Still, I'm sure there are kids in Darfur or Rwanda who would have been happy to be only tired and frustrated — as my mother loved to remind us when we were children — and could do with the warm meals we had. But when you were ten years old and lonely, you don't really care about some other group of kids a world away who probably would never have to deal with parents as vile and unforgiving as yours are. You just want it all to go away like I did on that bench outside the Sentinel.

My brother pulled up to the curb in his Vette and beckoned me into the car. "Where are we going and what the hell happened to you?"

"Take me to the nearest Dot's," I said. "Lots and lots of ice cream."

TWO

We walked into the ice cream shop that triples as a fast food restaurant and a grocery store. (In case you're wondering, this is how all Dot's ice cream shops are designed. It is the Walmart of fast food.) We were greeted by a metal-mouth teenager, dressed in Dot's green, purple and blue who looked entirely too perky for her own good. Her name tag read, "Pippy-Ann." I shit you not.

"Welcome to Dot's. May I take your order?" she said through her metal-induced lisp.

"I want ice cream," I said. My face was set. My hands were shaking. But neither of these ticks seemed to come across to this teen.

"What kind of ice cream would you like?" Pippy-Ann said without missing a beat. "We have exotic flavors like butter pecan, black walnut, fudge ripple, cherry amaretto, chocolate marsh—"

"I just want some ice cream."

"Oh, not an exotic ice cream connoisseur, huh? Well, in that case, we have home-style vanilla, chocolate, strawberry, cookies 'n' cream—"

"Look," I said, leaning close enough for her to smell my breath, "all I want is for you to go back there behind that glass counter, scoop out two scoops of ice cream, put it in a bowl and give it to me."

Pippy-Ann pulled back, frightened. Ron stepped in front of me and took over ordering. I found a vacant booth and sat down. I stared at the salt and pepper shakers, wondering whether either of them had ever been fired. I wondered how the salt and pepper shakers would have reacted to news of losing their jobs as the go-to guys for adding flavor and spice to an otherwise unfulfilling bacon cheeseburger. Would they have contemplated going back to the place they had previously depended on to supply their livelihood with a high-caliber rifle and seek retribution? Would they have contemplated the end of the world as they knew it?

Ron sat down across from me with a tray of goodies in hand. He put a burger, a shake and two scoops of ice cream in front of me. He proved he really was my big brother by making sure it was my favorite flavor. (Chocolate, in case you were wondering.) He bought himself the same thing, except he was a vanilla kind of guy. I stared at him for a moment, not touching my food, and he did the same to me.

"All right, little brother," Ron said. "This had better be good because you probably traumatized that poor girl back there for life. This is probably her summer job for Christ's sake."

I picked up a spoon and ate a bite of my chocolate ice cream. It wasn't as good as I hoped it would be.

"You have to talk to me, Mikey. No one has heard from you since yesterday and the picnic is tomorrow. Mom is worried about you again, and that means I have to lie to her and tell her you're okay. And you know I'm a terrible liar."

I took a sip of my milkshake. I felt the same way I had after eating the ice cream.

"Goddamnit, Mikey, talk to me. I'm your big brother. Who are you going to talk to when things get bad if not me?"

"Fiona."

"Okay, fair enough, but Fiona's not here. I am. So tell me what happened?"

I sat up at the table and glared at him again. He looked sincere. So I told him what had happened with Constance and at the Sentinel. His response: "Oh, you're so totally fucked."

Captain Obvious to the rescue.

"Thank you, Ron. I didn't know that until you pointed it out, but I'm glad to know you're still as observant as you've ever been."

"I'm sorry, but it's true. You haven't talked with your wife. You slept with another woman, and you lost your job. And correct me if I'm wrong here, but you're still without a car, aren't you?"

"No, I just called you for a ride because I love having these uplifting brotherly talks with you."

"Hey, you don't love the stripper, too, do you?"

"Now what the hell does that question have to do with anything I just told you?"

"Nothing, but you're dodging the question, which means you're thinking about it. Why would you need to think about it if the answer is definitely no? If you didn't think you loved her, you would have just said so. It's only logical. It took you years of harassment to finally jump in the sack with June. But it only took you, what, two days to bang the stripper. And let's face it, Mikey, when it comes to sex, you're a lot like a woman — you think of sex a lifetime contract sealed in sweat, coochy juice and semen. So you must think you might love her on some level at least, right?"

Sometimes it's scary to watch my brother's mind work.

"I . . . Maybe . . . I don't want to think about it. All I want to know right now is how I'm supposed to get another job before the picnic tomorrow and what I'm going to say to my wife. What am I going to do? I can't throw a football the length of a foursquare court. I can't rope cattle or put out fires. I can't rap. I can't even properly cheat on my taxes."

Ron bit into his burger and began chewing.

"This is the part where you're supposed to offer up some great big brother advice," I said.

"I'm thinking," Ron said through a mouth full of burger. He swallowed and then made a motion like he was Sherlock Holmes coming to some great conclusion. "You need to talk to June. I think you need to tell her about your car and losing your job and all about the stripper—"

"Constance."

"Whatever. I think you need to tell June everything. Come clean, and let the truth set you free — or some such shit like that."

Once those words left his mouth, I knew he was out of his fucking mind. "You're out of your fucking mind. The last time June saw me she told me not to come home, and that she was going to abort our firstborn. You think telling her I lost my job, and that I had sex with another woman, a woman she clearly detests, is going to fix things?"

"Eh, when she said all of that she was on the maternity ward of a hospital, pregnant, and you walked in with a stripper on your arm, a stripper I told you to leave in the truck. June's hormones were raging. She was bound to act out."

"This is my wife you're talking about, Ron, not some teenage girl who's daddy didn't love her enough."

"You're making my point. She's a hip chick, an understanding woman. I think if you just talk to her, she'll come 'round."

I looked at him skeptically. "Where is this newfound faith in June coming from all of a sudden?"

"What can I say? I'm a big enough man to admit I want you, my little brother, to be happy, especially after all the shit you've been through in the past couple of days. You always loved this girl, and if she loves you even half as much as you love her, she'll understand."

Sometimes, I really love my big brother.

"Are you gonna finish that?" he said. "That shit cost $6.57, you know."

And sometimes, I really hate him.

Ron finished his food — and mine — and convinced me to let him drive me home. All I could think about was whether or not there were any objects in my apartment that could be used as weapons against me. I didn't own a gun or a baseball bat. I didn't have any sort of pepper spray or mace. I had a lot of books, but nothing thick enough to be swung at me. But then I remembered the kitchen, and that the kitchen held knives. If June was pissed at me when I walked into the apartment, it was more than likely that no one would ever hear from me again.

Ron parked his car a few spaces away from my building, even though the space closest to where my apartment was located was vacant.

"Why are you parking here?" I asked. "That space up there is empty."

"If your woman is pissed, I don't want her coming anywhere near my baby," Ron said, patting the dashboard. "I won't allow my car to be the collateral damage of your fuck-up."

"What happened to wanting me to be happy?"

"I do want you to be happy. I just don't want my car scratched, keyed or vandalized in any way if June isn't. I'll stay here in case you need to make a run for it though."

"Thanks."

"What are big brothers for?"

I gingerly stepped out of the car and made my way toward my apartment. I stopped in front of the apartment door and said a Hailmary — just to be safe — crossed myself and then stuck my key in the door and unlocked it. I turned the doorknob slowly, thinking if I came in slow I might be able to duck an otherwise unseen fit of fury from my wife. I looked around the living room, and saw that no one was there. I called out June's name. Still nothing. I checked the kitchen, then the bathroom and finally the bedroom. I was the only person in my apartment.

I shut and locked my apartment door. I walked back to my brother's car and plopped down into the passenger seat.

"Did she threaten to chop off your dick?" Ron said. "Mary-Katherine did that once when she thought I was looking at her issue of Vogue for too long."

"She wasn't there. No one was home."

"Oh, well, we have to find her."

Again, stating the obvious.

"I know," I said.

"Where do you think she might be?"

I checked my watch. June usually worked until four o'clock at school. "She's probably at West Norman High. Her fifth period is her planning hour. If we hurry we can catch her."

"I forgot she teaches out there in the boonies."

"Ron, I live in Norman, Oklahoma. It's all the boonies."

"Maybe, but that new high school is still out in the sticks compared to the rest this place. Are you sure we have to go out there?"

"This was your idea to begin with."

"Fine, I'm going. I'm going."

Ron started the car and took Chautauqua to Highway-9 toward Interstate-35. He drove at a speed a little faster than I was comfortable with, but what do you expect from a man nearing his midlife crisis, driving a vintage muscle car. He took Tecumseh to Flood Avenue, and we were in front of the school building in less than ten minutes. My brother missed his calling as an Indy racecar driver.

Ron told me he would wait for me in the car, so I stepped out all on my own and made my way to the front gate of the high school. Rent-A-Cop with a flashlight on his hip stopped me there.

"Halt," Rent-A-Cop said. "I need to see some I.D., and I'll have to wand ya."

"That's not really necessary," I said. "I'm just popping in to see my wife."

"I don't care if you're the governor herself, I still need to see some I.D., and I'll have to wand ya."

I sighed and showed him my driver's license. He took my wallet in his hand and gave it the kind of thoughtful inspection a jeweler gives a minutely flawed diamond, and then gave it back to me.

"Empty your pockets onto the table," he said, pointing to a cheap plastic table behind him, "and hold out your arms and spread your legs."

I emptied my pockets and assumed the position. He brushed the metal detector up, down and around my body — twice through my crotch alone. "Satisfied?" I asked.

"For now," Rent-A-Cop said. "Be sure and check-in with the office before you even think about walking through my hallways."

Christ, you would have thought I was dealing with Wyatt Earp.

I nodded my head and made straight for June's classroom. It was toward the back of the school on the second floor. Her classroom wasn't so much a classroom as it was just a wide open space with wooden floors and lots of mirrors. There was a long steel pole bolted to the wall where I had seen June's students performing some really sadistic stretches. In the back of the classroom was her desk, where she kept a photo of us and a few scattered papers. I called out for her, but the only thing in her classroom was me and my reflection. I looked around a little while longer and then I left, thinking maybe the Mrs. Stratford would know where June might be.

I headed for the school's administrative office and was surprised to see how empty it was. Usually the office was filled with bad kids and worst parents, complaining about such things like organic milk being served at lunch. "My kid doesn't need to drink that hippy organic shit," one burly camouflage-capped dad once said. "Whole milk will get it done." Another parent once complained about the activities the P.E. teacher decided to employ during gym class. "Dodge ball should be outlawed in this country," the mother said. "No child should be subjected to that kind of persecution." But none of them were in today, and I was happy to see Mrs. Stratford was alone.

I said hello, and she popped her head up. "Oh, Michael McNulty, what are you doing here? I would have thought you would be at that *other* school talking to the next athlete who will throw away an opportunity for a top flight education for a little money and a convertible."

Mrs. Stratford could have been the long lost sister of Angela Lansbury. From her well-made-up skirt, blouse and jacket to her cherry red lips and blonde hair, this woman screamed school secretary. Oh yeah, she hates everything about Stark High School.

"Oh, no ma'am," I said. "I'm actually just looking for June. She wasn't in her classroom. This is her planning hour, correct?"

Her face looked confused. "Yes, it is, but June hasn't shown up the past two days. I would have thought you, being her husband, would have known that. Then again, you are a product of that *other* high school."

"She hasn't been in at all in the last two days?"

"No, she hasn't. We've had a dreadful substitute filling in for her. She smells like a skunk sprayed her and her eyes are always bloodshot and drooping. I have never met a lazier woman in my life."

"Okay, Mrs. Stratford, thank you."

I left the office, but I took the back way out of the school this time. I wanted to avoid Rent-A-Cop if I could. I went around back, ignoring a couple kids and what looked like an older, female adult hitting a bong.

Ron was standing outside his car, smoking a cigarette and talking to a girl who couldn't have been older than seventeen. "All right, Wooderson, get your ass in the car," I said. "And you," I said, pointing at the girl, "Go hit on one of your teachers."

"Damn it, Mikey, I was just trying to see if I still got it."

"You've got a wife and kids and mortgage. You don't need it anymore. In fact, you should put it away or consider having it removed."

Ron shook his head and threw away his cigarette. "So, what'd your old lady say, ye of the cock-blocking wisdom."

"She wasn't there."

"She wasn't at school. Now you're not only married to a baby-killer, you're married to deadbeat. What kind of lower-middle class wife doesn't show up to her fucking job?"

"Mary-Katherine doesn't work."

"Mary-Katherine is a lot of things, but lower-middle class ain't one of them. Don't ever confuse me with some other penniless big brother you might have who is derelict in his duties to you from time to time. I'm *rich* and derelict in my duties. There's a difference."

We hopped into the car, and Ron turned the ignition, bringing in some much needed air-conditioning. "So where do you think she is?" he said.

"The only other place I think she could be is at her parent's house."

"Where do they live?"

"Noble."

"Around by mom and dad?"

"No, Mr. Summers owns about six hundred acres across town from mom and dad."

"What's he do?"

"He raises cattle. What else is man with six hundred acres of cleared land in central Oklahoma going to do?"

"Put up some kick-ass condominiums and prefabricated homes. Can you think of anywhere else she might be?"

"Nope, if she isn't there or her parents don't know where she is, I don't know where else to look."

"Thank God."

I gave him an exasperated look.

"Oh, sorry, it's just all this running around is starting to get on my nerves."

THREE

Bob Summers' land sat on some of the hilliest property I have ever seen, and his house was situated the apex of the highest hill. I had been out there many times before and even managed to screw up the courage to stay the night once or twice. And each time I was overwhelmed by the beauty that surrounded me. Waking up to sunrises without the whine of cars and trains, watching sunsets without the glare of street lights — that was magic to me.

Every time I had ever been out to the Summers' land I had come graciously and with the timidity of a child. I wanted to be a great guest, courteous in the presence of my then fiancée's parents and make the kind of good impression all perspective suitors do. But not this time. This time I was going beat down the door until someone answered — like I was S.W.A.T. or something — and demand to see my wife. Damn the impression. Damn my natural timidity in their presence. It was getting to be Zero Hour.

"You want to go alone?" Ron said.

"It's probably best that way."

"Good, I heard these black farmers got shotguns."

"Ron, this is Oklahoma. Everyone has a shotgun."

"Yeah, well, I'm not getting shot for your—"

"Yeah, yeah, you told me already. I'll see you back here."

I took in the size of the Summers' house. It seemed bigger than I remembered, but I think a wraparound porch will summon that illusion. Still, the house seemed darker and more intimidating than I can recall. I took it slow up the steps to the door. I wasn't in a hurry at all. In fact, I'm pretty sure a slug passed me by on the way. I came to the door, steadied myself and then took a deep breath. I had pulled back my fist to knock on the screen door when the wooden door behind it slowly swung open.

"Mikey," Mr. Summers said. "I thought you'd be around sooner or later." He pushed open the screen door.

"Yes, sir," I said. "I'm looking for June."

He nodded. "She's riding. I suspect she'll be back in about a half-hour or so." He waved his hand at me. "Come on in, son. You can wait in the living room with me until she gets back."

I followed Mr. Summers into his house, checking to see if any firearms were within arm's reach. He pointed to his couch. "Sit down," he said. "You want something to drink? Sweet tea? Beer?"

"No, sir, I'm fine." I gingerly sat down on the cotton couch.

Mr. Summers poured himself a glass of tea and sat down in his recliner across from me. He rocked back and forth, staring at me for a few minutes.

"Is Mrs. Summers home?"

"Nope. Rebecca is in Oklahoma City, doing some shopping at some new outlet mall out there. It's just me and you."

Okay, that last sentence, I could have done without.

"Neat," I said.

"How's work?"

"Work?"

"Your job at the paper?"

"Oh, it's good. It's fine. I'm fine. Everything is fine."

"That bad, huh?"

I smiled sheepishly. "Yes, sir."

"Do you want to talk about it?"

"With all due respect, Mr. Summers, I'd like to talk with June about it before I talk with you about it."

He smiled. "I respect that. But you should know if June doesn't tell you what you want to hear, it's not necessarily a reflection on you as a husband. But if she tells you what you need to hear, you should probably heed her advice. Understand?"

"Yes, sir."

Mr. Summers stood up and walked toward me. "You're not a bad man. You're just in a tight spot is all. You have to do the best you can for you." He patted me on the shoulder and walked away from view.

I watched the clock for a little while, trying to guess how long I had been waiting on June when I saw her outside the sliding door in the living room that led to the largest part of Mr. Summers' land. She was jumping off of her horse and making her way toward the screen door. She was dressed in cowboy boots, blue jeans, a white tank-top and a ten-gallon hat. I had only seen her dressed like that a few times before. But each time I did, she looked even more beautiful.

I stood up from the couch and faced the door. She saw me and put her head down. She walked toward the door and let herself in.

"We need to talk," I said.

June pulled off her gloves and looked at me. "I know," she said. "We do. Wait here. I'm going to go take a shower."

"You didn't have to come all the way out here, did you?"

"This is my family."

"I'm your family too." I moved in to kiss her on the cheek, but she moved her head before I could. She walked past me and into the hallway that led to her bedroom.

I paced the living room waiting on her, thinking about where I would start, and how I was going to justify my actions. If I sound to you like a small child who's trying to come up with a reasonable way to tell mommy her vase shouldn't have been in the way of my soccer ball, we have nothing more to discuss on the subject of my emotions. Still, the reality of what I was about to tell my wife was beginning to become a little bit more than I could bear. I sat down on the couch, twiddling my thumbs and watching the clock.

June came down the hallway, dressed in her favorite purple and pink pajamas. Her hair was still wet around her shoulders. She sat down on the couch next to me.

"I need to—"

"I want a divorce," June broke in.

I felt a sudden pain in my stomach.

"This isn't working," she said. "This isn't what I wanted. This isn't how I envisioned this would work. I love you. I have always loved you, but now I see I was right to call the wedding off in the first place. I don't love you like I should a lover. I love you like I would love my brother or best friend. You have always been my best friend."

I felt warm tears beginning to roll down my cheeks, though to this day I would swear there was something in my eye — both of them.

June reached for my hand, but I pulled it back. I didn't want to be touched just then, by her or anyone else.

"Talk, say something," June said.

"Are you still going to, uh, not have the baby?"

June pulled back and set her face. "I made an appointment in Oklahoma City. I'm going tomorrow. I don't expect you to come with me."

I nodded as if I understood, but I didn't. "Can I ask why?"

"You can ask."

"Why aren't you having the baby?"

"There's more of life I haven't seen, we haven't seen. I'm not ready to give up a life I barely started; not yet. I want to travel. I want to dance. I want to—"

"And you can't do all of that with me and a baby?"

"I knew you wouldn't understand. You've always been so fucking *Catholic*. It was cute when you were in high school, and God knows my parents loved that I was best friends with a boy who wouldn't ever have sex with me. The world is bigger than your Bible and your commandments and your Catholic rhetoric — and I want to see just how big it is. I can't do that with you—"

"Or a baby."

I never knew I wanted the chance to be a father until that moment; the moment I knew June was taking that chance from me. I couldn't fault her for having dreams, for wanting a bigger life. I just never thought those dreams and a marriage and child with me were mutually exclusive.

"Do you think we could start over?" I said. "I'd like to try this again. I think I can do it better this time. We can have way more sex."

June frowned. "You'll find what you're looking for one day, Mikey."

"But I—"

"You're not getting it, Mikey." She sighed and then cut her eyes at me. "The baby isn't even yours. It's Jake's."

"Jake's? Jake Mishkin's?"

"Yes."

"But you told me you never had sex with him. You told me you were just panicked. You told me you were just testing me."

"I lied."

Fuck me.

"I wasn't about to tell the man I thought I wanted to spend the rest of my life with that I had cheated on him before we were even married."

"So you lied to me twice about Jake?"

"I didn't think I'd have to do it more than once."

"Does he know?"

"He came into town yesterday. He's going with me to the clinic, and then I'm going to move to New York with him."

Okay, that sucker punch wasn't even called for. I was already emotionally drained when I walked into her father's house, but if I wasn't that knowledge torpedoed whatever optimism I had left.

"So it's not that you don't want that life. It's that you want a life with Jake. In New York."

"I have some auditions at some really great companies lined up. This is the chance of a lifetime for me."

I stood up and started toward the door, but I only made it as far as the end of the couch and turned around to face June. "Over the past two days, I've had some really bad shit happen to me. The highlight was watching my father disown me right after you left on the elevator at the hospital where my sister gave birth to my newest nephew. My car has decided to quit on me. I lost my job this morning, and all I could think about was how I was going to explain this all to you. But now I see that all pales in comparison to what you said to me not two minutes ago. Oh yeah, one more thing, I did sleep with Constance, but only after you told me not to come home to my apartment."

I left June sitting on the couch and went out the door to my brother's car. He was sitting with the car running. His paranoia borders on hilarity.

"Well I sure hope she was home because I'm not driving your ass anywhere else," my brother said. "You were in there forever."

"She was there," I said.

"Good, how did it go? Does she want your testicles in jar?"

"She wants a divorce, and she's having the abortion."

"Damn, little brother. I didn't think she'd go that far."

"She went further."

"How did she do that?"

"The kid I've been obsessing over for the past two days? She said it isn't mine."

Ron grew silent. We both stared at the cows on the Summers' land through the windshield. The sun was beginning to set.

"Mom called while you were in there with . . . uh . . . her. She wanted to know if the picnic was still on."

"Yes," I said. "The picnic is definitely on."

"But what about June? She isn't still coming, is—"

"I said the picnic is on."

"You want to go out for a drink?"

"No, just take me home, Ron. Just take me home."

FOUR

Ron banged on my apartment door. "Mikey, open this door," he said. "I swear to Christ if I have to tell mom you hung yourself from the ceiling fan, I'm going to make it look like you were jerking off before it happened. We might as well go for national news."

I came to the door and opened it. "Stop yelling," I said, plopping down on the couch in my living room. "I haven't killed myself, not yet anyway."

Ron stood over me. "Maybe, but you look like the walking dead and this after just one night alone. You don't take bad news well, little brother."

He was right. I was in my boxers and v-neck undershirt. I hadn't showered or shaved in two days, and for me, that's about as long as it takes for me to grow a hobo beard and fester a funk that would make me look and smell homeless. "Did you bring coffee?" I asked.

"It's one o'clock in the afternoon. It's a little late for coffee, don't you think?"

"It's never too late for coffee."

"Now you sound like dad."

"What?"

"You know, he would always say it was never too late or too early for a drink."

"Yeah, well, no amount of coffee ever made me angry enough to smack my second-born around like a fucking piñata."

"I'm sorry. I shouldn't have said that."

"He's the least of my troubles."

"I'll make you a pot of coffee," Ron said, walking into my kitchen. I heard him poking around in my cabinets for a little while before he said, "Mikey, where is your coffee pot?"

I labored up from my couch. My couch had this habit of sinking into the ground if anyone sat on it for longer than five seconds. But it wasn't bad considering I dumpster-dove to get it.

I looked around my kitchen for a few moments and then it donned on me. "June took it," I said.

"That bitch took your coffee pot?"

"Actually, it wasn't mine. We threw mine out for her piece of shit. The fucking thing had an alarm clock. What kind of sick human being puts an alarm clock on a coffee pot?"

"Damn, Mikey, what else of yours did you let her throw away?"

"A lot. I thought I was doing, you know, good husband shit."

Ron nodded as if he knew exactly what I was talking about, and for once, I think he did. "Have you looked around to see what else she took with her?"

"I haven't had time to wallow in the loss of material shit."

"What do you mean? What did you do all of last night because you clearly weren't sleeping?"

"I killed some aliens and saved the world. Did you know you could save the world from the invasion of a perceived more intelligent and technologically advanced race in less than six hours of game-play?"

"You're telling me the way you thought best to cope with all the crap that has happened to you over the past two days was to play video games? That's the best self-destructive behavior you can think of?"

"I haven't showered either," I said defensively.

"You have to get dressed now. Mom and the rest are expecting us in less than an hour, although I don't know why since we're the only family showing up. You still want to go through with this?"

"Yes, I do. I'll go put on some clothes and we can leave."

"Oh, no you won't," Ron said. "First, you're going to take a shower and shave. Then we can go into public without anyone thinking I'm chauffeuring the Unabomber around."

I took a shower and shaved, though I didn't feel better afterward. I felt fake and disingenuous; at least my filth and unkemptness reflected the way I felt inside. I pulled on a pair of jeans, a white shirt and my tennis shoes and presented myself to my brother. "Better now?"

"Yes, much," Ron said. "Let's go."

Immediately, the heat and humidity of the day struck me hard in the face. Only my mother would think it was a good idea to have a picnic at midday in July in Oklahoma.

"So what are you going to tell mom about June and the rest?" Ron said, speeding down Chautauqua.

"I'm thinking."

I actually was thinking about what I might do, what I might say to mom as well as the rest of the family. With any luck my brother knew better than to break the bad news himself, spilling his guts to anyone with the last name McNulty. But that would only serve to make the shock value of what I said nuclear. My mother would probably faint regardless, but the measure of just how much I had failed would undoubtedly be expressed in Pappy's reaction. The man is a human barometer of fucked-up-ed-ness.

"Is dad coming?" I asked Ron.

He looked at me and then back at the road. "No, I don't think he is."

"Well that's one less disappointed face I have to endure."

"I still don't get it," Ron said. "Why haven't you just called the picnic off? You could have done this yesterday at mom and dad's and saved us all the grief of cooking like roasted turkeys in the sun."

"Because the park is a neutral field and bad news is more manageable on a full stomach."

"Whatever, Mikey," Ron said, shaking his head. "I hope you know what you're doing."

"I do." Or at least, I thought I did.

"What about mom? Has she mentioned June?"

"Nope, she's been acting like nothing ever happened, not even her fainting at the hospital."

That did not sound like my mother. "Why hasn't she said anything?"

"Probably because of the oxytocin."

"Mom's on oxytocin?"

"Well, technically, she's on three happy drugs — oxytocin, lithium and Xanax. She has been for a few months now. She went to see Dr. Schwartz not long after you told her you married June. I guess she couldn't take it."

"How did I not know this?"

"You haven't been paying attention, not that I blame you. You've been dealing with a lot of shit lately. She's increased the dosage too."

This explained a lot. This explained my mother's sudden kinship with June and her want to be congenial — even motherly — with us all. My mother was always on edge, but it was something I became used to as a kid and didn't think about as an adult. "What do you mean she increased the dosage?" I said.

"I mean, before she was just taking the dosage her shrink ordered. But lately, she's been popping those pills like breath mints."

Great, my mother was already a borderline alcoholic and was now on the verge of becoming a drug addict.

We came to Griffin Park sooner than I had expected we would, but then again I could probably throw a rock from my building and hit some dude playing disc golf at Griffin. Norman is a small city. Ron pulled up to where my family had set up shop. There was a large red and white table cloth draped across a moderately-sized wooden table under a gazebo. My mother was making herself busy, setting the table with plates and utensils. I looked around and saw two coolers and three large platters of tinfoil on the ground nearby.

Ron and I stepped out of the car and descended on the family. I cut a beeline for Fiona who was holding her son in her arms. My brother's two kids, Ronnie and Paula, and he hugged and kissed them like the loving father we never had.

"Are you all right?" Fiona asked. "You don't look so good."

"Whatever happens at the table later, just go with it, okay?" I said.

Fiona narrowed her eyes at me. "Mikey, what happened after you left the hospital the other day?"

"I promise I'll explain everything at the table."

"Where's June? Where are the Summers'?"

"At the table, Fiona."

Fiona made her I-don't-like-this-but-I'll-go-along-with-it-for-now face and started back toward the table.

Ron's kids suddenly looked up from their dad and slammed into me, enclosing themselves around my legs.

Ronnie pulled back. "Hey uncle Mikey," he said, smiling from ear to ear. Paula looked up at me. "Daddy says you've been having a really hard time this week, and we're supposed to hug you and give you kisses until you feel better."

"He did, did he?" I said. I looked at my brother. He threw his hands up in surrender.

I bent down on one knee and took my nephew and niece into a large hug, and they kissed me on the cheek. "I love you, uncle Mikey," Paula said. "Me too," Ronnie said.

"I love you both too," I said and hugged them again.

They turned and ran to the table. As they did, I felt jealous of my brother again. I was jealous of what he had and what I may never have.

Mary-Katherine patted her kids on their heads as they passed by her and stopped in front of me. "So, where is this black woman my husband says you married?" Mary-Katherine said. "Tell me she is at least Catholic."

As you can tell, my brother chose a wife as close to the living likeness of our mother as humanly possible without the help of a cloning agency. And naturally, my mother loved her. Me? I treated her like a sister-in-law most of the time — someone I (begrudgingly) tolerated on holidays and family functions, nothing more nothing less. But that day marked the beginning of something new.

"Yes, Mary-Katherine," I said, "my wife is black. She will contaminate the McNulty gene pool with her blackness and Southern Baptist ways. I think I'll even give a name to the hybrid strain of children we'll conceive. I'll call it, Disappointing My Family And My Brother's Bitch Wife."

"There's no need to be hostile. I just thought you would have had the good sense not to marry one of them."

"I told my brother the same thing about you."

The woman named for a Drexel saint cut her eyes at me and grew tiny red horns atop her head.

"You're a bad apple, Michael McNulty."

"The worst," I said.

Mary-Katherine turned away and headed toward the table. I was checking my pockets for a cigarette when I realized I didn't have any. So now I was going to have to deliver my news without the calming affects of nicotine or the hyperactive affects of caffeine. This was not part of my original plan. I started walking toward the gazebo while taking in the fact that I was going to be completely sober while delivering the news of my ending marriage to my mother when I heard his fucking name.

"Jake," my mother said from under the gazebo. "It's so nice to see you."

Jake — the Antichrist — walked right by me. He fell into the warm embrace of the one who mercifully shat me from her womb after twenty-seven hours of labor.

"How are you, Mrs. M?" the Antichrist said. "You don't look a day over twenty-five."

Can you believe that? The Antichrist was hitting on my mother right in front of me.

"Michael," my mother said, "come say hello to Jake. He came in town just for this picnic."

I suppressed the urge to power bomb the Antichrist right on top of my mother's well-laid table and mustered up a "Sure thing, mom." I sauntered toward the table and took a seat next to Pappy, who became perturbed anytime he was outside — no matter the event. The Pope could be staging a prayer day at Memorial Stadium, and my Pappy wouldn't go unless the Pope himself guaranteed the outdoor stadium would be air-conditioned.

"Good Christ, it's hot," Pappy said. I sat down next to him.

"Don't take the Lord's name in vain," my mother scolded.

"God made this day hotter than the metal hinges of Hell. That makes us even."

The rest of my family sat down at the set table. Judging from the amount of food on the table, my mother had done yeoman's work: hamburgers, bratwurst, sausage, chicken, baked beans, sweet potatoes, yellow squash, wheat rolls and enough sweet tea to fill a large bath tub. The Antichrist had the nerve to sit directly across from me. I knew someone would postulate where June and her family were, and I was praying to God it wouldn't be my mother.

"Michael, where is June and her family?" my mother asked.

God is a spiteful bitch.

"I think we should eat, mom," I said.

"I came all the way out here in the blazing sun to break bread with these savages," Pappy said. "Now where the hell *are* they?"

I sighed, took a deep breath and said, "They're not coming."

"Just like darkies," Pappy said. "They have no sense of other people's time. Here I am, cooking in this wooden sauna, and I won't even get the satisfaction of examining these spooks for myself."

"Well," my mother said. "They could have done us the courtesy of calling to cancel in advance. And after all the trouble June and I went through to put this together. This is very disappointing. Did they at least say why?"

"I think we should all have something to eat first, mom, really," I said.

"Michael, just tell us all why they're not coming to the picnic. It's hot enough without your stalling."

"There are actually quite a few reasons why they might not be coming," I said. "They might not be coming because I got fired from my job yesterday. Or they might not be coming because my wife told me — her ultra-Catholic husband — she was having an abortion the same day my baby sister gave birth to a son she named after me. They even might not be coming because I slept with a beautiful stripper named after a saint. But I think they're most likely not coming because June and I are getting a divorce because she had sex with that asshole sitting right across from me."

The entire table became silent — even Pappy. Looks were exchanged between everyone at the table. My mother turned a deep shade of red, then purple, and then — on cue — fainted in her seat. My brother jumped out of his seat and tended to my mother, but I held the Antichrist's gaze. He looked petrified. I leaned across the table and threw a right cross for the ages that landed on the Antichrist's bulbous nose. The Antichrist keeled over out of his seat on the ground, holding his nose, which spilled blood like it was being poured from an open faucet.

"Holy shit," Pappy said.

"Ditto," Ronnie and Paula said in unison. Their jaws were slack and their mouths looked like something akin to a largemouth bass out of water.

I walked over the table, straddle him and began raining down fists. Before I knew it, my brother was pulling me off of him, and my knuckles were bloody. The Antichrist stood up and ran away. I could hear Mary-Katherine cackling behind me as I watched my brother go back to my mother. She slowly came to, and Ron leaned her up so that she and I were face to face.

My mother looked stunned and disoriented. She looked up at Ron and then back at me. We sat silently for a few more moments, and then she said, "How much of what I thought I heard you say is actually true?"

"All of it, ma," I said. "It's all true."

"You really got fired?"

"Yes, ma'am."

"You slept with a stripper?"

"Yes, ma'am."

"She's really having an abortion?"

"Uh-huh."

"You're really getting a divorce?"

"Yes, ma'am."

"And Jake really is having an affair with June?"

"Uh-huh."

"Oh, okay then. Someone will have to let your father know," she said. And then she commenced crying.

"Well, all this could have been said at home, if you ask me," Pappy said. "Now, not only do I have a grandson who has been stood up by a darkie — not once but *twice* — and left with more sins than any citizen of Gomorrah, but this entire family is going to Hell in hand basket. If any of you dreaded seed of my seed need me, I'll be in the car with the *air-conditioning* on, trying to think of how I'm going to explain away this shitstorm to Saint Peter at the gates." Pappy stood up, slowly waddled toward my mother's purse on the table and drew out her keys. I watched as he disappeared from view, cursing under his breath.

My sister gave my nephew to Mary-Katherine, sat down next to my mother and held her while she cried. Mary-Katherine, who had stopped laughing when she realized the severity of the situation, took my nephew and her kids to the nearby playground. My brother sat down next to me and produced a of pack cigarettes. He handed me one, and we smoked to the sound of my mother's tears for few minutes.

"You know, if I had known this was what you had in mind, I would have never knocked on your door today," Ron said.

"I'd say I'm sorry, but I'm not," I said.

"Hand me mom's bag," Fiona said.

I reached up above me and pulled down mom's purse from the table. I handed it to Fiona. She rummaged through it and pulled out a bejeweled pillbox. She took a pill out and fed it to my mother. My mom took it down dry.

"You knew about this?" I said to Fiona, pointing to my still sobbing mother.

"Of course," Fiona said. "Dad took to drinking early on to cope. Ma has her pills now."

"Cope? Cope with what?"

"Life, Mikey; it's not what they expected either."

Leave it to my baby sister to be the philosophical and emotional linchpin of my fucked up family.

My mother quit crying and was able to hold it together long enough to help me and my siblings clean up the beautiful spread she had lain out. She was smiling and humming as she worked, picking up uneaten food and taking random swigs of sweet tea straight from the pitcher. The woman was scaring me.

"How long has the humming and smiling been going on?" I asked, helping Ron fold the table cloth in two.

"Since she started taking her meds," Ron said.

"And you're both all right with this?"

"Think of the alternative," Fiona said. "Do you prefer hysterically sobbing, spiteful vindictive mom to this slightly over-medicated happier version?"

I stopped mid-fold with Ron and looked at my mother. She traipsed around the picnic table, humming to herself. "Well, no, but this version can't last, can it?"

"As long as the world keeps producing happy drugs it can," Ron said.

We finished folding the picnic cloth and Ron left Fiona and me to go see about his wife and kids and nephew. I sat down on the picnic table and watched as my mother continued to clean up. Fiona sat down next to me.

"Now, are we going to talk about what the hell is going on, or are you going to give me some B.S.?" Fiona said.

I put my head in my hands and then fell over into Fiona's lap. "It's all falling apart," I said. "It's all just falling down around me."

Fiona stroked my hair. "First, it's not all falling down around you. You've still got me. You've still got Ron. We're here, and we're not going anywhere. Second, I'm sorry."

"You're sorry? For what?"

"For June. If I hadn't said what I said to you when I was about to pop with my son, you probably would've never married her in the first place."

"You didn't make me marry her. I did that all on my own. Besides, I backed out of it too. My instincts were screaming at me, and I ignored every last one. And for what? A bout of sex? Well, several bouts of sex. But still."

"Yes and what's this business about you having sex with a stripper?"

"It all happened kind of fast. I don't even remember most of it. All that remains is my hangover and the feeling of waking up naked with my pants around my ankles in high grass."

"Sounds kinky."

"Not funny, Fiona."

"It's a little funny. Do you love her?"

I looked up from her lap. "What kind of question is that? Mom is five feet away."

"Mom is on drugs, and you haven't answered the question."

"How can I love someone who I've known for all of three days and has threatened to dislodge my testicles from my scrotum on more than one occasion?"

"That's not a no."

"You and Ron are both the same."

"So he thinks you must love her too, huh?"

I rose up from Fiona's lap. "Why don't either of you think I'm capable of casual sex?"

"Because you aren't. You're not an unattractive man, Mikey. You may think so, but most women would disagree. And in one way or another you've passed on all of them with the exception of June and now the strip—"

"Constance," I interrupted.

"Yes, Constance. You must feel something for her. And Dad. You still need to talk to dad, Mikey."

"I'm going to find Ron. I think it's time for me to go home."

"Mikey I didn't mean—"

"Let it go, Fiona. I'll talk to you later."

I kissed her on the cheek and moved toward my mother at the other end of the table. I kissed my mother on the cheek. She barely noticed me through her golden smile and humming. I started walking toward the playground, looking for my brother. I didn't want to think about Constance, June or any woman.

I found Ron near the swing set, watching his kids smile and laugh on the jungle gym. "Can you take me home?" I said.

Ron faced me and asked, "Are you okay?"

"I just want to go home."

"Okay, I'll take you home."

FIVE

Ron and I were silent on the way back to my apartment. I didn't feel like talking, and he knew better than to ask me again if I was okay. He shut off the engine and turned to me. "Did Fiona talk to you about him?" Ron said.

I didn't even need to know who "him" was. I already knew. "You two conspired together on this?"

He sighed. "We only want you and dad to make peace with each other. That's all. You make it sound like we're committing treason against the country?"

"You are."

"What?"

"You are committing treason against the country, against the country of us — the kids, the three siblings. You're supposed to be on my side."

"Mikey—"

I threw open the door and leapt out of the car before he could utter another word. I heard the window roll down. "Fine," Ron said. "Be a horse's ass."

I heard the Vette turnover and roar out of the parking lot. I never looked back. I sauntered toward my apartment door. I stuck my key in and heard her familiar voice behind me. I turned around. "What do you want?" I said.

"I want to talk to you," Constance said.

She was dressed in torn blue jeans, charcoal cowboy boots and a purple shirt with the word Dancer written across the chest in bold, pink letters. Her hair was down around her shoulders.

"I was all ready to talk to you when I came out of confession. But then I had to walk to work where I found I no longer have a job and my wife doesn't want to be my wife anymore."

"June left you?"

"Like it's a big deal to you. Now that you know my life is in the shitter, we don't have anything left to talk about."

"Yes we do. We have to talk about what happened the other night. That's not something I usually do with a guy . . . well ever."

"You did it at least once before. He must have been pretty good at it, too, to get you to marry him — a regular pro."

"That's not fair. You don't even know what I felt then. You don't know what I feel now. For you."

"Fine, why don't you tell me then?" I folded my arms and leaned against my apartment door.

"Before, I was just learning who I was. I was just learning what I wanted when this boy came along. He told me he loved me, and at eighteen, that's all any girl wants to hear from a cute smart boy. So when he asked me to marry him, I didn't even think about it. I just thought it was all a fairytale, even the part where we got married in Vegas. But I've learned since then. I didn't love Jake. I love you."

"Jake? Jake who?"

"What does it matter? I just said I love you. That's the big deal here."

"Jake *who?*" I said through clinched teeth.

Constance lowered her head and said, "Jake Mishkin."

Fuck.

"You married Jake Mishkin?"

"Well I'm not married to him anymore and I came to tell you . . . what I told you and that I am moving to San Diego. I won't say it to another man, and I promise this will be the last time I say it to you." She walked closer to me and placed a folded piece of paper into my hands. "This is where I'll be in San Diego for awhile. You can call me or write or whatever."

"Is that all?" I said.

"No." Constance leaned in and kissed me on the lips. I didn't kiss her back. I crumpled up the piece of paper in my hand and watched as she turned her back and walked away.

Maybe I should have called out to her and asked her any one of the hundreds of questions that were running through my mind. Maybe I should have taken her in my arms and kissed her — with tongue — and poured my heart out to her. But I didn't. I just watched her walk away. Why? Because I was angry. I was angry at the world and everything in it. But most of all, I was angry at God. I had done it all by the book with minor slipups here and there. And all I got in return was my heart crushed, my job taken, a car that committed suicide and a father who would have rather disowned me than talk about our problems. I had had it.

I opened the door to my apartment and threw Constance's crumpled note on my desk. I saw my rosary beads on the coffee table. I picked them up and threw them against the wall. I sat down on my couch, fuming. Then, all of a sudden, I wanted to talk to someone. But I didn't want to talk to any of my siblings or my parents. I didn't want to talk to Father Jacob. I wanted to talk to someone who had no real knowledge of what had gone on in my life in the past four months. But most of all I wanted to talk to someone who would listen, really listen to what I had to say; to my side of things. I opened the door and started walking.

The entire trek took me about thirty minutes from my apartment, and I was sweating profusely by the time I arrived there. But I wasn't at all disappointed by who was working the cash register at Brown Stain that evening.

"Dream quitter," Steve shouted. "Back for another Bold Pick of the Day or caffé mocha? Or is it the espresso and chocolate chip cookie today?"

I leaned across the cash register so I was just inches from Steve's face.

"Whoa, dream quitter," he said. "You've got a scandalous look in your eye."

"Can we smoke?" I said.

"I would, but I gotta close tonight and—"

I grabbed him by his green Brown Stain apron and pulled him close. "You said if I ever needed to talk to anyone, I could come to you. Here. I. Am."

"Okay, okay, calm down, dream quitter. I can see you're a man in need. Meet me out back behind the store in a sec, okay? I gotta put one of my underlings on the register."

I left the store to go around back. In a few moments, Steve was outside with a small pipe, a lighter, a sheet of cardboard and a plastic bag of weed in hand. He beckoned me over and we leaned against the brick wall and slid down to a seated position.

"So, why are we about to get brutally faded and gloriously baked on this hellaciously hot evening, dream quitter?"

I watched as he meticulously laid out his cardboard and situated all of the necessary items just so on it. If I didn't know better, I would have said the man was getting ready to perform heart surgery.

"Woman problems," I said. "Well, woman problems, job problems, family problems and car problems."

Steve shook his head knowingly. "All right, I'm good at all of those things . . . except the car part. I hate cars."

"How do you get to work every day?"

"I ride a Vespa."

"You ride a scooter?"

"No, it's not fucking a scooter. It's a Vespa — a scooter *with class*."

Steve carefully packed the pipe with weed all the way to the brim. He lit it and took a long drag before he passed it to me. I hit hard, too hard. I started coughing enough to provoke Steve to pat me on the back.

"Virgin lungs? You look like you might've hit the peace pipe before."

"No," I said with a chest full of smoke. "I smoke. I've just never smoked weed before."

"This isn't just weed, man. This is *Haze*. I broke out my top-selling shit for you."

I coughed again. "You're a dealer?"

"Of course, dream quitter. Working at Brown Stain doesn't even cover my fucking monthly Vespa payments."

"But I thought you were working on a novel?"

"I'm not working on it. It's finished. I'm still waiting on an agent with the balls to put my manifesto in the hands of a publisher."

"How long is it?"

"About nineteen hundred pages. It's better to keep it light for a first book, or so I read on some dude's blog once. Anyway, tell me about your job problems first. I think that's a good place to start."

"Okay," I said, passing him back the pipe. "I lost it."

"Lost what?"

"My job."

"Bummer. No more TPS reports for you to do, huh?"

"I was a newspaper reporter."

"A shit-shiller. My old man is a shit shiller."

"Oh yeah, anybody I know?"

"His name's Ellis, Merlin Ellis."

Talk about your holy shit moments.

"He was my boss. Or my boss' boss at the Sentinel. I liked him."

"He's a good enough guy, yeah. He was excited when I told him I was going to major in English, but less so when I turned to selling Mr. Haze. We're still amiable though."

"Do you think you can help me get my job back?"

"We're not *that* amiable. What else you got, dream quitter?"

"How about family problems? My dad disowned me, and I just found out my mother has been on drugs for the past four months."

"It's not meth, is it?"

"No, it's not meth."

"Good, switching to that shit totally robbed my bro, Perkins, of a decent livelihood."

"Was he an addict?"

"No, he was a dealer. That shit's hard to move, man."

"Right. Well, do you have any advice about how I can make things better with my parents?"

"The drugs your mom's on? Do they make her a better mommy? Like, does she function better?"

I actually gave this serious thought before answering. "Well, she seems to be much happier when she's on them, but—"

"Are they legal?"

"Yeah, but—"

"Then leave the lady her drugs. And if she ever decides to take up the peace pipe," Steve said, pointing to smoke flowing from his own pipe, "be a good bro and send her my way."

"What about my dad?"

"He need to score some good ganja?"

"What should I do about working stuff out with him?"

"Oh. I don't know. Have you tried talking to him?"

"Not lately, no."

"Then talk to him. He's your old man, which makes him half you. It can't be that hard to talk you. I'm doing it, and I'm fine."

"You don't understand. My dad is an asshole."

Steve laughed through a hit and passed me the pipe. "And you think you're not an asshole?"

"Well, no. I don't."

"That about makes it official then, doesn't it?"

"But I'm not an asshole. I'm not a bad person."

"I'll bet your old man doesn't think he's such a bad dude either, dude. Just try to talk to him."

"And if that doesn't work?"

"Then you can always take up smoking the Jolly Green Giant's stalk like the rest of us. Now the women — the women are the easiest problems to solve."

"Okay, but first let's see if I can't summon a buzz," I said. I took a long drag off the pipe and nearly choked on the hot smoke.

"You gotta learn to take it easy with the Haze. This shit is some biblically powerful shit."

I coughed a little more and settled myself before spilling the goods about June and Constance. Steve's initial response: Taking another long drag on his pipe. And then another.

Finally, Steve said, "Have you killed this guy Jake Mishkin yet? I know a guy who knows a guy who owes me a favor."

Just so we're straight. So not only is Steve a barista at Brown Stain and drug dealer, he knows men who know hitmen.

"I told you I got him in the nose pretty good," I said.

"Yeah, I heard you, but that kind of betrayal deserves a distinctly violent form of retribution."

"It's fine. I'm fine now."

"No, we're bros now, dream quitter. We have shared the peace pipe. This is a solid I must do for you." Steve's eyes showed a special glaze, but I let it go.

"What do I do about my wife?"

"Wait, she's the bitch who ditched you for this hairy ball sack named Mishkin, right?"

"Something like that, yeah."

"Fuck her. You don't need her. Let her go on doing whatever she thinks is right for her."

"Just let her go? Just let what we had go?"

"Unless you want to have your nuts forcibly removed from your body again, yes. That chick has some bad juju headed her way."

"How do you know?"

"I don't. Haze does. Haze knows all. But this other chick—"

"Constance," I said.

"She really said she loved you after one date."

"Yeah, she did, sort of. Why, what do you think?"

"I think she's either psychotic or genuine. Problem is the psychotic ones always seem genuine. Is she stalking you?"

"No, not really. She's moving to San Diego though. I don't know."

"I know. Stalkers never leave their prey. I had this one chick literally sleep outside my dorm room for five weeks before the cops finally took her away. I ate the girl out just once, and that's what I got for my stellar fellate skills. Yeah, dream quitter, I think she loves you."

"Really?"

"Yeah, really."

"But she—"

"She loves you, bro."

"And I—"

"She loves you, man. Get over it. The only question is whether or not you love her?"

"I don't know if I love her or not."

"Of course you do."

"How do you know?"

"Would we really be wasting Haze on a chick you don't love if you had just hit it and quit it? I don't think so. Dudes don't obsess over the one night stands. They obsess over the women they wished they had owned up to loving before it was too late."

"But I barely know her."

"And she barely knows you, yet she still told you she loved you. The chick's got guts. But you? You're just a dream quitter who wouldn't own up to loving someone who loved you because it was something new."

He was right. I had let what was right in front of me get away. Or did I? I stood up, and started walking away.

"Hey, where are you going?"

"To find Constance."

"Okay, don't worry about that Mishkin fuck. Revenge shall be yours, dream quitter."

SIX

The sun was on its way to bed, and I was sure the crazies and drunks were about to descend upon Chesty's, but I didn't care. I had to find Constance, and coincidentally — not coincidentally at all, if we're being honest — I was hungry. But I couldn't stop either. I decided it was best to just keep walking down Asp until I came to Chesty's and hope I would find her there. But oddly enough, there was a line outside of Chesty's that seemed to go on for at least two blocks north of the strip club.

I came to the velvet rope outside the club, manned by a black guy who couldn't have been taller than 5-foot-3, but he had arms bigger than his legs. I tapped him on his bulging shoulder, and he turned around to look up at me through his darken sunglasses. "End of the line, pot head," he said and turned around. I smelled myself, then checked my reflection in the glass outside the club. My eyes were blood shot, and I reeked.

I tapped him on the shoulder again.

"What?"

"I'm just looking for a friend," I said. "I just need to know if she's in there."

"Buddy, the only women in there are the ones with singles in their g-strings, and unless you're in line and can pay the cover, I can't let you in."

"But you don't understand. I'm just looking for a friend. I'll be two minutes."

"Is your friend one of the dancers?"

"Yes."

"No chance."

Why didn't I just lie to him?

"Okay, what's the cover charge? I'll pay it right now."

"Fifty bucks."

"Fifty bucks? Who do you have in there? Jenna Jameson?"

"Tonight's the only night Ms. Lily the Midget Stripper will be in Norman, and as you can see, she's a draw."

I took out fifty bucks and handed it to him. "Here," I said. "Take it, and let me in."

"No can do, Smokey."

"Why not? You said all I had to do was pay the cover. This is me paying it."

"I said you have to get in line and *then* pay the cover."

"C'mon, you seem like a nice little fellow—"

The bouncer punched me in the crotch, and I fell on the ground.

"I've had it with you alcoholics and druggies making fun of me because I'm short. Now pick your sorry, smell lanky ass up and take it to the end of the line before I stomp a mud hole in you."

I slowly picked myself up. "You wouldn't have a candy bar or something, would you? I'm starving." The bouncer pointed toward the line. I nodded and started walking. I came to the end of the line right around the Cookies and Whipped Cream bake shop. They were closed. God is a spiteful bitch. I stayed in line for nearly two hours while listening to the two guys in front of me go on and on about Ms. Lily's superhuman dexterity. When I finally came to the front of the line I tried to apologize to the bouncer, but he just took my money and acted as if I hadn't apologized at all.

The club looked just as packed inside as it was outside. I could barely move through the leagues of men who all seemed to be gravitating toward center stage. My curiosity led me to at least try to catch a glimpse of this wonder midget I had now heard so much about. (She has been known to abuse overzealous fans with a nightstick she uses as a stage prop. She can twist her body into the resemblance of an actual bow and arrow and her zodiac sign is Taurus.) I watched as she performed several acrobatic somersaults and handstands, which led me to believe she also was a hardcore gymnast in her youth. My reason for being in the club kicked in as I was watching her — along with the need to feed my grumbling stomach — and I started toward the bar. I squeezed in between two men and was able to find an empty stool at the counter. I pulled a bowl of bar nuts in front of me and commenced shoveling the salty legumes into my mouth by the handful.

"Hey, this ain't no charity bar," I heard. "You're gonna eat my nuts, you gotta buy a drink."

Ordinarily I'd have made a That's What She Said joke right there, but in the interest of my own life I decided to refrain. The voice came from the bartender, who looked to be at least three hundred pounds.

"Sorry," I said. "I'm just so hungry."

"I don't care if you're an Ethiopian refugee dying of starvation. You want to eat my nuts, you gotta buy a drink."

You should laugh. I wanted to.

"I'll have a . . . a shot of Jack Daniels."

The bartender placed a shot glass on the counter and poured. I took it down, feeling the fire all the way to my near-empty stomach.

"You want another one?" he said.

"No, I'm just here looking for a friend. Maybe you can help me?"

"I don't have any friends." There was not one ounce of ha-ha in his expression.

"Okay, but maybe you could help me find my friend?"

His facial expression didn't change, so I continued. "Her name is Constance. She works here."

"Are you one of those stalkers?"

"Who? Me? No, I'm just looking for her because . . . I just need to talk to her."

"You *are* a stalker, aren't you?"

"No, I'm not a stalker. I just think . . . I just think I love her. That's all."

"I'm calling the cops."

"Don't do that. Can you just tell her I'm here? That's all. If she says she doesn't want to see me, then I'll leave. Just tell her I'm here, okay?"

The bartender eyed me, then he turned and walked away. I sunk in my stool and laid my forehead down on the counter. I didn't want to think about what would happen if she didn't want to see me. I didn't want to think about what would happen if I was wrong to have taken her seriously in the first place. I was in a club — a strip club — claiming to be in love with a stripper. They have rooms reserved at mental institutions — and sometimes, prison cells — for people like me.

I felt a tap on my head. I looked and saw a beautiful young brunette in laced lingerie staring at me. "Who are you?" she said.

"I'm Mikey. Who are you?"

"I'm Glamorous, a friend of Constance."

Yes, I can vouch for the glamorous part.

"Is she coming to talk to me?" I said.

"Are you a stalker?"

"Why is everyone obsessed with calling me a stalker in this place?"

"We get a lot of them here. But you never answered the question."

"No, I'm not stalking Constance. Will you answer my question?"

"No."

"Why not?"

"I meant, no, she's not coming out here to talk to you."

"Did she say why?"

"No, she didn't."

"Why not?"

"She's not here. She picked up her check this afternoon and said something about leaving for San Pedro or something."

"San Diego?"

"Yeah, that's the place. How'd you know?"

"Never mind. What else did she say?"

"Nothing. But she was crying. Something about how stupid she was to love some guy. I told her. All men are dogs. They can't help it. No offense."

"None taken. Did she say anything else?"

"There was just a lot more crying. No man is worth even one tear if you ask me." Glamorous turned and strutted away.

I stood up from the bar, feeling lower than when I first walked in — a feat I didn't know was possible until that moment — and worked my way through the crowd toward the exit. No one was outside waiting to enter the club. The streets were sparse with pedestrians but full of cars. I assumed many people were having a good time. Some were having a nice family dinner. Others were having a night out with friends. But not me. I was alone. I walked home with my hands in my pockets, praying June hadn't taken all of the microwave dinners with her when she left me.

Three Weeks Later

SEVEN

No, I still hadn't fixed my car in case you were wondering. But I had moved from my couch to my kitchen and to the bathroom once or twice. I also moved on from killing aliens to playing football and soccer on my TV. It turns out playing video games is like most other things: If you work at it, you'll get better at it. It's not like fucking (with) the wrong woman. There, I can't help you. No one can. After all the fiery hoops I've been made to jump through, I only wished I had never met a woman in my entire life. Not my mother, not my sister, not Constance and damn sure not June. This probably means I wished I had never been born as well. So be it. That's about where I was when I heard a knock at my door.

I scratched myself out of need — something else had started growing around my crotch, and it wasn't hair — and leaned off the couch. I opened the door and saw my baby sister holding a baby bag in one hand. My nephew's infant jaws were wrapped around her bigger-than-ever breast. Naturally, I flinched.

"I really didn't need to see that."

"Shut up," Fiona said, walking past me into the living room. "It's not as if you haven't seen a woman's breast before."

"Not with a baby bearing my name attached to one, I haven't."

"Oh, get over yourself. He'll be done in a minute." Fiona took in what my apartment had become. "This is an ungodly mess."

"It's just as well then, isn't it?"

"Why?"

"There is no God."

Fiona rolled her eyes and brushed off some leftover pizza I had on the coffee table off. She sat down. "You should really stop being so melodramatic about all of this. Worst things have happened."

"Not to me they haven't."

"You're overreacting, as usual."

I slumped down on my couch across from Fiona and folded my arms. "Tell me, Fiona, how am I overreacting?"

"Well for one thing, no one has seen you in weeks—"

"Funny, that's what happens when someone doesn't want to be seen ever—"

"And for another," Fiona continued, "It's not like you were in the best emotional state to handle June or Constance, let alone on the same day."

"Oh, not the psychoanalysis again?"

"Hey, buster, you called me."

"That was two weeks ago."

"And I haven't stopped thinking about you since then."

"So you're going to start in with the psychoanalysis, huh?"

Fiona pursed her lips, then her eyes became the size of saucers followed by a loud gasp.

"Fiona?" I said. "Fiona, are you okay?"

She let out a low sigh. "Yeah, I'm fine. He just bit me is all," she said, gesturing toward the baby.

"Is he done yet? I mean, surely the kid can eat some other time, right?"

Fiona gave me a stern look.

"Fine, continue with the feeding," I said. "I'll just watch the little vampire have at you from two feet away."

"I'll throw something over him. Will that make you more comfortable?"

"Much. This borders on porn for me. And with my sister, that's not cool."

Fiona took out a quilt and threw it over top of the baby. She left an opening for his head to peek out while he fed.

"I know that quilt. That's mom's quilt. She used to wrap it around me when I was feeling sick or had just puked."

"I've washed it many times for that reason."

"Why are you here, Fiona?"

She ignored the question. "Jake is in the hospital. He said he was jumped by a bunch of guys dressed in black track suits outside the Brown Stain on Campus Corner."

"Did they break anything?"

"Yeah, actually. They broke three of his ribs, but I don't think that's what he's still in the hospital for. Mom said something about his suffering third degree burns on his face and torso. I think she said someone poured coffee over him."

I let a faint smile slip. Fiona didn't notice.

"Ron, Mary-Katherine and the kids are fine too," Fiona said. "They said they tried to call, but you didn't answer. You haven't returned anyone's phone calls."

"I've been busy."

Fiona ignored the malice in my voice and continued talking. "Mom's good, too. She's worried about you."

"If she's so worried, why didn't she come with you to make sure I'm still breathing?"

"You know why."

"She's still taking his side, huh?"

"Dad was her husband before he was your father."

"And that makes it all right?"

"No, but it should help explain why she is acting the way she is."

"It doesn't. Besides, isn't that what the drugs are for?"

"C'mon, Mikey, she's in a tough spot. Can't you understand that? She shouldn't be made to pick between her son and her husband. Not by you, not by anybody."

"And you? Is that how you feel too?"

"I'm here, aren't I?"

I smiled and looked at the large bump slowly heaving under my mother's quilt. "May I hold him?" I asked.

Fiona nodded. She took off the blanket and gently placed my nephew in my arms. "He's bigger than I remember," I said, still looking at my nephew.

"That's what the doctor said, too. I think he's going to be something great, just like his uncle."

"What are you talking about? I haven't done anything worthwhile since the day I was born."

"You're doing it right now, Mikey. You're doing something great for me, for your nephew. You're doing more right now for him than his father has or ever will. You might not think it's a great big deal, but it is. It really is."

I smiled at my baby sister and turned my attention back to my nephew. Staring into his green eyes, I knew what I needed to do. "I'm going to try to fix things between the old man and me, sis. And then I'm going to leave. Will you take me to see Father Jacob?"

"Sure. But where are you going to go?"

"San Diego."

"What's in San Diego?"

"Constance."

We loaded into my mother's car, and Fiona drove me to St. Mary's. I hoped Father Jacob was in his office. I stepped out of the car. "I won't be long," I said.

"Take as much time as you need," Fiona said. "We will be out here waiting for you when you get back."

I walked into the church and paid my respects to The Emaciated One upon entering. I was about to take the staircase to Father Jacob's office when I noticed his silhouette in the first pew near the altar. I ventured toward the pew and took a seat next to him. He kept his gaze on the altar.

"I haven't seen you at mass lately."

"That's because I haven't been coming, Father."

"No one has seen much of you from what I understand."

"I haven't wanted to be seen."

He turned in his seat and faced me. "You do not have the look of a man who is at peace with God, my son."

I laughed. "How very astute, Father."

He furrowed his brow.

"I'm sorry, father. I just don't feel like God and I have anything to discuss. Our relationship has changed."

"Your relationship with Him may have changed, but His relationship with you has not. I can assure you of that."

"Can you, Father? Can you really say God is still on good terms with me, that He loves me the way you have said He loves us all?"

"Yes, I can."

"What evidence do you have? And no, I am not interested in faith today. I'm not interested in what you believe could be true, only what *is* true."

Father Jacob pulled back in his seat. I could see him thinking. He reached out for my hand. "Let us pray."

I pulled back my hand and shook my head. "No, Father."

"But I am just going to ask the Lord to—"

"Ask him yourself, Father. I didn't come here to pray with you."

"Then why did you?"

"I came to ask you to watch over my sister and her son like you watched over me."

"Of course I will. But I would have done that even without your asking."

"Thank you, but I just had to be sure. I don't know that my parents are equipped to help raise another child, and I won't be here to help Fiona along."

"Where are you going?"

"I'm going to write. I am going to find out what I believe outside of this church, outside of this town."

Father Jacob smiled. "Constance loves you, too," he said. "She told me so that day."

I smiled. "Thank you, Father."

We stood and Father Jacob embraced me in a hug. "You will still pray every once in awhile, won't you?"

"I promise to find out what I believe, and not just what you and the church have taught me."

He nodded. "Then I will see you again?"

"Not for some time. But my family is here. Fiona and my nephew are here. I think I'll find a way to come back."

"I will pray for you."

I nodded my thanks and turned my attention toward The Emaciated One. I stared at the Son of God for a few moments, and just as I was about to turn my back on Him, I thought I saw Him smile at me. Yes, I think He did smile at me that day. I was about to cross myself, but I stopped and just smiled back.

Outside I heard the car running. I jumped into it and felt the freezing temperature on my skin. Fiona had the air-conditioning blasting. "Cold enough for you?"

"You're crazy if you think I'm going to let this blazing heat anywhere near my son," Fiona said. "It's bad enough that he'll have to stay here until I get my shit together. How did it go?"

"It went well."

"Did you tell Father Jacob that you're leaving?"

"He knows."

"And did you tell him the reason you're leaving?"

"He knows that too."

"All right then," my sister said gleefully. "Where to now?"

"Home."

"You want me to take you back to your apartment?"

"No." I turned to face her. "I want you to take me home."

Fiona smiled and shifted the car into gear.

EIGHT

The ride to my parent's house was mostly quiet, save the rhymes from Lupe Fiasco on the radio. (God bless my baby sister for knowing my taste in music.) Occasionally, I checked on my nephew in the backseat. But for the most part I just stared out the window, taking in what I was going to leave behind. I hadn't been back to my parents' house since the day I told them June and I weren't getting married. The truth: I never wanted to go back after that day ever again. But it turns out I have a conscience, and no matter how much I fight it, I care what that racist codger I call my father thinks. Maybe you knew this all along. Maybe you didn't. But it doesn't matter now, does it? It only matters that I left my sister in the car again to knock on my parents' door.

My mother answered the door and wrapped me in the kind of hug I had wished she was capable of ten years ago. She stepped back and delivered a smile I had previously thought could only be shown with the help of an extensive amount of electrolysis and Botox. She hugged me again and then showed me into the house, past The Emaciated One and into the living room.

"Would you like a cookie, Michael? I really want to bake you some cookies." That smile was still there — and it was starting to creep me out.

"Mom, are you okay?"

"I'm fine. I feel great."

Over her shoulder, I saw an assortment of pill bottles with prescription labels across them. It had taken that long for me to remember. Instead of confronting her about her grief, about how she was really feeling, I chose to take the advice of the coffee Nazi and drug dealer. I left her in her happy place.

"Yes, mom," I said. "I would love a cookie."

"Good, I'll bake you a bunch."

My mother left me in the living room and set herself about the work of making cookies — from scratch. My mother never made anything from scratch. We're talking about a woman who once thought heating up a frozen chicken was more of hassle than it should be. Drugs are powerful shit.

I paced around the living room for awhile, taking in the pictures of my siblings and me growing up through the years. I was amazed by just how different we looked back then. My brother was the tall one in the family right up until he left for college. I only caught and surpassed him two years later. My being tall was always something I never got used to — I had been short for too long. I stopped at a photo of Fiona. She looked so young just four years ago. Now she seemed like she had aged twenty years. I guess that's about right — you don't become the wise baby sister without some battle scars, and she had suffered many.

I heard a grunt behind me and turned around. My father held a half empty glass of Jameson's in his hand. His eyes were red and sullen. He didn't look happy to see me.

"What the fuck are you doing here?" he said.

See? I was right.

"I need to talk to you," I said.

"You're not mine anymore. You need to leave before I break my foot off in your trespassing ass."

I could smell the Jameson's seeping through his pores from three feet away. "Okay," I said. "You're drunk, so I'll leave." I turned to walk away, but I realized I might not have that chance ever again. I may not have ever been able to talk to my father again. I stopped and approached him until I was just inches from his face.

"What?" My father spat the words into my face.

"To say my peace," I said.

"I don't want to hear anything you've got to say." He turned his back on me. I reached out, grabbing his shoulder. He spun on me and launched his glass at me. I ducked it, falling to the ground. I heard the glass shatter against the wall. He kicked at me on the ground but missed. The force of his swing left him unbalanced, and he crashed to the floor in a heap on top of his shoulder. I stood over him and watched as he grabbed his arm in pain.

"You done?" I asked.

My father didn't move, didn't answer. He just lay still on the ground.

"Good. Now, first, I am your son; blood of your blood, flesh of your flesh, bone of your marrow. Once upon a time, I didn't like knowing that anymore than you do right now. Everything about us is different. I used to think the only thing we shared in common was our last name, and then I realized why that one piece of my identity, of your identity, means so much to you. It meant so much to you that when you thought I had sullied it for good, you hit me. That's nothing new in this father-son relationship. But I can see now that you were more hurt than angry. And at the hospital, you let that anger lead you down this path. Okay. I get that. I helped this relationship get to this point. But damn, dad, all you had to do was tell me you loved me. Even after what you said about June and all the things you ever said and did to me, I would have let it all go without thinking twice if you could have just said those three words to me. And if I hadn't recently planned to leave this patch of red dirt, I might be able to let things between you and me fester and rot for the rest of my life. But I'm not staying here. I'm leaving, and I probably won't see you again for a long time. So this is it. I love you, dad, even if you still don't love me."

I stared at my father, waiting for a response. And I waited, and I waited. Nothing. He only stared at me.

My mother suddenly appeared — in an apron no less. "I heard a ruckus," she said. "Are you both all right?"

I looked at my father and then turned to my mother. "Mom, I think I'm going to have to eat those cookies another time." I left the house and jumped back into the icy car with my sister and nephew.

"How did it go?"

"It was me trying to end a 23-year-old feud with dad," I said. "How do you think it went?"

Fiona nodded and backed out of the driveway.

NINE

I packed only the things I needed, or thought I needed: my laptop, my cell phone, J.M. Coetzee's *Elizabeth Costello*, *The Brief Wondrous Life of Oscar Wao* and a few pieces of clothes. I closed out what was left of my life savings and junked my car for pennies on the dollar. It was just as well — after seven years as my bitch that car had earned its death. I used half of my severance to pay off some things, and the other half I had either used to buy a bus ticket or pocketed to help me on my way to San Diego.

I heard two knocks at the door. I opened it without looking. It could only be one person. "Are you ready to go?" Fiona said. She stood alone in the doorway with a plate of chocolate chip cookies in her hands.

"For me?"

"Yeah, mom said you left them yesterday."

I chuckled to myself. I took the plate from her and set it on the coffee table. I grabbed Constance's note off my desk and then my bag on the ground next to my couch. I took one last look around my still mostly-furnished apartment. "Yeah," I said. "I'm ready."

She nodded, issuing her somber approval. I followed her out of the apartment and locked the door. We stepped into the car, and I watched as my sister started my mom's car and steered it onto the road.

"Mom hasn't minded you taking her car?" I asked

"Mom's drugged to the bejeezus. She doesn't even know she has a car."

"You know where you're going, right?"

"Yes, I know where I'm going."

"I was just checking."

"You're not doing this because of me, are you?"

"Doing what?"

"Going to San Diego?"

"Is this a trick question?"

"No, I just . . . I just gave you bad advice about the other one, and I don't want to feel responsible if she turns out to a philandering cunt like the other one."

"Did you just call June a cunt?"

Fiona peeled her eyes from the road for a moment and looked at me. "Well, she is, isn't she?"

I laughed. "I don't hold you responsible for my decisions, not with June, not with Constance and certainly not with me leaving."

Fiona smiled and pulled into the Greyhound parking lot.

"You don't have to do this," Fiona said. "We can go right back to your apartment and think up a new, more grounded plan."

I laughed. "This coming from you?"

"I'm serious. Chasing this girl may not end the way — no, strike that — it probably won't end the way you think it will."

"I know it might not, but how can I truly know for sure if I don't try?"

"Have you even thought about what you're going to do when you get there? Do you even know where to look for her?"

I gripped the crumpled note in my hand tighter. "I've got a pretty good idea."

"And that's enough for you?"

"Yes." I didn't even have to think about the answer. The word was there as if it had been patiently waiting to leave my mouth for so long. I reached into my bag and pulled out a thick envelope and placed it into my baby sister's lap.

"What's this?" she said.

"Open it."

Fiona fingered the envelope open and gasped.

"There's about five grand in there," I said, "and the keys to my apartment. Don't worry about paying rent for the next six months. I already took care of it. I know you think it's a pigsty, but it could be a place for you and my nephew to stay for awhile. You know, until you get back on your feet."

Fiona hugged me tight. As she pulled back, I saw tears in her eyes for the first time in years. "I love you, Mikey. You had better take care of yourself and write me at least once a week."

"You're welcome."

Fiona wiped the tears away from her blushing face and turned her stern face on again. "I still don't know why you're riding the bus," she said. "There is a perfectly good airport in Oklahoma City."

"I need time to outline, time to think and scenery watch. Plus, it was about four grand cheaper to ride the bus than fly."

"You're going to finish your novel?"

"No. I'm going to start a new one."

Fiona smiled at me, and we stepped out of the car together. I presented myself at the cashier's desk and completed the final necessary and mundane activity that placed my life in my hands. I hugged my baby sister and watched her drive away.

A shrill voice came over the intercom and instructed myself and others to board the bus. I walked toward the back and found a window seat. I stuffed my bag in the overhead storage compartment and waited for the bus to finish boarding.

An old man in suspenders and a fisherman's hat sat down next to me and nodded. "Where are you off to, young man?"

"I'm going to California."

"To see about a girl?"

"Yes sir. To see about a girl."

"Is she worth it?"

I smiled. "She had damn well better be, or I'll have to write an entirely different story."

Made in the USA
Charleston, SC
10 May 2012